Crazy HEARTS

AMBER KELLY

Cover Design: Sommer Stein, Perfect Pear Creative Covers
Cover Image: Michaela Mangum, Michaela Mangum Photography
Editor: Jovana Shirley, Unforeseen Editing, www.unforeseenediting.com
Proofreader: Judy Zweifel, Judy's Proofreading
Formatter: Champagne Book Design

To Julia, a great friend and kick-ass woman, who knows the joy and heartbreak that accompanies the journey to motherhood. You make it look so easy.

Crazy
HEARTS

Prologue

CHARLOTTE
Three Years Earlier

I'M EXCITED AS I LOOK AROUND THE CAMPSITE. ALL OF SOPHIE'S new and old friends are here. I've never been camping before. I know what it is, and I've seen it on television and in movies, but I've just never done it myself.

I knew visiting Poplar Falls was going to be an adventure. I researched ranches online before I arrived and read an entire article about a dude ranch in Montana. It sounded like a dream. It's what I expected to find when I landed in Colorado, but that's not what I got.

Sophie explained dude ranches are commercialized ranches that are created to be tourist vacation spots, catering to Yankees looking for a country living experience. Rustic Peak is a full-fledged true cattle ranch and not a fantasy vacation for city folk.

Honestly, I couldn't care less because for this city girl, it is precisely what I was hoping for. Hot, hardworking cowboys with calloused hands, brooding attitudes, and big hearts with large, supportive families and small-town charm. It's better than I imagined. Especially in the *hot cowboy* department.

"How are you holding up?" Dallas's brother, Payne, asks as he plops down in a lawn chair beside me.

"Me? I'm having a blast," I tell him.

"Really? I would have thought this would be too outdoorsy for your liking," he says.

"Granted, eating beans out of a Styrofoam cup and drinking illegally made grain alcohol aren't my usual Saturday night activities, but I didn't travel two thousand miles for normal," I explain.

He chuckles. It's a deep rumble, and I like the sound. I turn to face him fully. He's handsome in a rugged way. His dark hair is tucked under an old ball cap; a button-up flannel is stretched tight across his massive chest, the sleeves pulled up to his elbows; and his jeans are well-worn and faded and fit him oh-so right. His stormy-gray eyes are framed by long lashes, and they are watching me intently.

"Are you sure you and Dallas are related?" I ask.

He raises an eyebrow at me. "Yeah. Why?"

I shrug.

"She's redheaded and tiny and you're all dark and massive and buff," I explain.

He scoots his chair closer to mine, and I'm suddenly enveloped in the most intoxicating scent of pine and spice and man.

"You think I'm dark and buff?"

I roll my eyes. "Like you don't know you give off all sorts of *sexy cowboy* vibes."

"I'm not doing anything on purpose, but if you think it's sexy, I'm not complaining."

"Is that so?"

"Yes, ma'am," he says.

I point at his mouth. "See, there you go again with that sexy talk."

He bites his lip to hold back a laugh, and I imagine sinking my teeth into that plump lip.

"Tell me, cowboy, are you single, or do you have some lucky girl waiting for you at home?"

"If she were at home while I was sitting here with you, would that be lucky?" he asks.

He's got me there.

I shake my head.

"Nope, but I feel pretty lucky," I tell him.

He moves in closer. "Is that right?"

I nod. "If you play your cards right, you just might be lucky too."

"Why do I get the impression that you are all kinds of trouble, sweetheart?"

"Instinct?" I answer, and he laughs.

We spend the rest of the evening drinking and talking. I tell him all about New York, and he fills me in on all the Poplar Falls gossip.

By the time the fire dies out and everyone else has retired to their tents, we feel like old friends.

I think I might have found that Colorado mountain adventure I was searching for.

Now, if I could only talk Dallas into switching tents.

One

CHARLOTTE

"**S**HIT."

My mother is standing in front of the swanky windows that overlook Times Square. She is dressed in a sleek one-shouldered black dress, and her blonde hair is in a smooth chignon.

Uh-oh.

She rarely curses. She finds it uncouth.

"What's wrong?" I ask as I hurry to her side.

I'm used to her being frazzled before her and my father's annual New Year's Eve party, which also serves as a fundraiser for the Feed the Children Foundation, a charity for which she sits on the board of directors. Philanthropy has been her passion ever since Mila, my younger sister, graduated seven years ago. Before then, she was a full-time mother and socialite, dedicated to being the perfect PTA and cheer mom, while my father worked his ass off as a trader on Wall Street to keep us all in the lap of luxury.

"The sommelier just canceled. Guests should be arriving any minute now, and he just called me," she shrieks.

"Why?" I ask.

She waves her hand around in the air, as if the answer doesn't matter. "Something about his wife and an accident or so-and-so. What do I do now?"

I place my hands on her shoulders to calm her and look her in the eyes. "Just breathe. It's fine. People have gone centuries drinking wine they picked out, opening and pouring it themselves. I know it's a hardship, but dammit, this is what we do when faced with a crisis of this caliber. We are Claiborne women, and we will pull up our big-girl panties and overcome this catastrophic event, come hell or high water. Now, point me toward those orphaned bottles of vino, and I'll handle this."

At my declaration, her expression goes from panicked to amused, and she melts into tense laughter.

"Oh, Charlotte, you know how much this event means to me. I know it's silly, but I just want it all to be perfect," she says.

"I understand, but, Mom, something always goes wrong. Last year, it was the caterer running late, and the year before, it was the piano player getting stuck in traffic. You can't control every little thing all the time. The party is going to be exquisite and raise tons of cash, as usual. I'll call my friend Andrew and offer him an absurd amount of money to drop his New Year's date and come fill in. He's a connoisseur of wine and the one I call anytime I need to be reminded of what wine is served with what food," I offer the solution before I walk toward the coat check to retrieve my cell.

"Tell him to bring the date. I'll waive the per-plate fee for her. Maybe getting to eat caviar and drink the finest champagne while watching the ball drop from above Times Square will keep him out of the doghouse," she calls after me.

I turn back at her and wink. "Yes, ma'am."

That's my mother. She might be high society, but she is no snob. She cares whether her temporary bartender still gets lucky tonight.

I exit the door to the ballroom and head for the entrance. The door to the powder room opens, and Mila emerges, fanning the puff of white smoke that follows behind her.

"Were you smoking in the restroom?" I ask as she falls in beside me.

"Maybe," she answers.

"I thought you quit. Those things will kill you, you know," I scold.

"I know, Mom," she says as she rolls her eyes.

I stop dead, and she looks back at me.

"You take that back," I sneer.

She huffs and gives in. "Fine, you're not as bad as Mom."

I purse my lips and continue forward.

"Where are we going anyway?" she asks.

"To get my phone. Mom has a staff crisis I need to solve quickly before she loses her shit," I fill her in.

"Great. I'm not going in there until Dad gets here, or all her focus will be on me. *Mila, your dress is too short. Mila, your eye makeup is too dark. Mila, did you get another tattoo?*"

"*Mila, why do you smell like a perfumy ashtray?*" I add.

"Exactly," she agrees.

"Where is Dad anyway?" I ask.

"He went to pick Alex up at the airport. They should be here any minute," she informs me as we reach the coat check closet. Alex is our older brother who now resides in Boston.

A perky brunette in a black blazer is standing behind the counter.

"I need my purse, please, Jane," I tell her, and she nods before disappearing behind the swinging doors.

Mila leans her hip against the desk and sighs.

She looks amazing in her wine-and-gold ombré-sequined cocktail dress that fits her body like a glove.

"Do you want to slip out with me later?" she asks as she bites at one of her nails.

I fight the urge to slap at her hand. "To go where?"

She gets a hopeful look in her eye. "I know of a great party in SoHo," she answers.

I'm tempted. In fact, I spent the better part of my twenties sneaking out of this shindig with my best friend, Sophia Lancaster, while our mothers were engaged with other guests. We would make it down to Times Square just in time to see the ball drop and kiss some handsome strangers before following the partygoers into one of the dance clubs. New York is a city that doesn't sleep in general, but at the beginning of a new year, it's an unending three-day celebration.

"Whose party?" I ask before I decide.

She shrugs.

"Someone Blake knows. He promises it will be full of celebrities and other glamorous people, but who knows? The music and crowd have to be better than here though."

Blake Thornton is a childhood friend. His mother and mine have been close since before we were born. We even dated briefly in our post-college days. I usually look forward to seeing him walk into one of these social events. He's a great dance partner and drinking pal, but I haven't spoken to him since before Christmas.

"I'd better not. I promised Mom I'd help her with the silent auction and stay till the bitter end, and I'm still on thin ice from skipping out on Christmas, so I don't want to press my luck," I answer.

"Suit yourself. You'll cover for me if she asks where I am though, right? If she misses me, just tell her the wine gave me a headache or something and I left to lie down."

"Sure. No way she'll see through that stealthy excuse," I say.

Jane returns with my silver clutch in hand. I thank her and walk back to my mother as I dial Andrew.

Please pick up.

4

The room is already filling with people dressed in expensive attire and dripping with jewels when my father and brother, Alex, finally walk in.

"There they are," Mom cries and waves her hand in the air to get their attention.

"Wow, look at you two handsome devils," I say as they make it to us.

Dad kisses me on the cheek before he wraps one arm around my mother's waist.

"We are hobos next to you two," Dad compliments, and my mother gives him her megawatt smile. "Shall we take a walk about the room, dear?" he asks.

"Yes, time to turn on that charm and get them to break out those checkbooks," Mom informs him.

"Of course," he says as he leads her into the crowd, leaving Alex and me to ourselves.

"Hi, big brother. Long time no see," I say as I grab a glass of champagne off a tray as a server snakes his way through the crowd.

"Too long, weren't you a redhead the last time we video-chatted?" he asks.

"Yeah, I dabbled on the wild side, just to see which really do have more fun." I shrug.

"I'm guessing blonde won?" he asks.

"Nope, turns out I have fun no matter what color my hair is."

"I have no doubt," he agrees.

Several of our parents' friends find their way over to say hello and to make small talk with Alex. It's like I'm invisible standing next to our family's new hotshot attorney. I don't mind though. I love my big brother. He is one of the best people I know. He was my first friend, protector and secret keeper growing up.

After about an hour of socializing, Mom takes a microphone

and speaks to the crowd, giving a little background info on the charity and the fundraising efforts of the night.

Alex shifts in closer to my side. "We're heading out soon, right? I can ask Dad to cause a distraction, so we can slip out." He slides his eyes to me.

"Where are we going?"

"Mila texted me about a party in SoHo."

"Of course she did. The little traitor plans to ditch as soon as she can," I grumble, as I turn up my glass and swallow the contents in one gulp.

"And you don't?" he asks.

"Ugh, no, thank you, and I don't think you should go either," I tell him.

"Why not?"

"Because Mila and her friends are into recreational fun that no big brother would approve of, and the last thing you want is to be dragging a kicking, screeching female out of a posh party."

"Oh God, what is she up to now?"

I shrug. "Nothing too hard core, but she's a fashion model in New York City. Partying is practically a job requirement, and I think her idea of partying and our idea of partying are slightly different."

"Shit, now, I definitely need to go," he mumbles.

"No, you don't. She's a big girl who can handle herself. What you need is a drink and to keep your favorite sister company."

I look around for a server to flag down more alcohol.

"How's Boston?" I ask.

Alex is two years older than me. He moved to Boston to attend Harvard Law School and decided to stay when he finished his degree.

"Cold. Same as here," he says.

"Mom hasn't talked you into moving back to Manhattan yet?"

"Not for a lack of trying, but no. I like where I am. New York is a shark tank for new attorneys. It's all about the old boys' club here," he says.

"And Boston's not?" I raise an eyebrow at him.

He smirks. "There might be a girl."

"I thought so. Spill," I demand as I take his wrist and drag him to the bar.

"She is the daughter of one of my firm's partners. It's casual for now, but I like her, and I want to see where it goes," he confesses.

"A partner's daughter, huh? You're not using this relationship to angle for a position, are you? Because that's just a douche move," I tell him.

"No. I didn't even know she was his daughter when we met. She was in the coffee shop around the corner from our building. We started chatting, and I got her contact info. It wasn't until a week later when I bumped into her outside her father's office that we put two and two together," he explains, offended by my question.

"Good. I didn't think you were that guy."

"What about you? Any man in your life?" he asks.

Payne Henderson's name is on the tip of my tongue. He is the man I've sort of been dating for a few years now.

Wow, has it really been that long?

He lives in Poplar Falls, Colorado, and I met him while visiting Sophie, who had gone to visit her hometown when her grandmother passed away and ended up never leaving. But I catch myself right before I spill it.

"Nope," I squeak out instead.

"What was that?" he asks.

I cough and take a less than graceful gulp from my glass before I slide my eyes away and ask, "What?"

He comes in closer and answers low, "Charlotte Claiborne, don't try that with me. You've never been able to lie to me. Ever."

I wrinkle my nose in frustration. He's right. Even when I could convince our parents of an exceptional tale, Alex would always have my number. Overprotective big brothers are such a buzzkill when you're in high school.

I look him straight in the eye as I clarify, "There's no one serious in my life at the moment. Honestly."

"You're not still doing that dating app thing, are you?" he asks.

"Hey, online dating is a perfectly normal way to meet people in the twenty-first century," I defend my dating past.

I went through a merry-go-round of potential partners over the years. Online dating is sort of like digging for the prize at the end of a cereal box when you were a kid. Sometimes, you got the cool secret decoder ring, and sometimes, you got a stupid plastic whistle.

"It is, but you have to date the man for more than a month to know if he's the one," he says.

"Who says I'm looking for the one? I like variety. Besides, you're beginning to sound like Mom and Vivian," I retort and then cringe.

Vivian Marshall is Sophie's mother. Alex used to date my best friend before he went away to school.

"How is Sophie these days?" he asks passively, but I can still see that glimmer in his eye.

He took their breakup pretty hard. It sucked, being the one in the middle of the drama. I hated seeing my brother's heart broken, but I knew Sophie never really fell for him the way he did her. She was too guarded back then.

"Married with a newborn," I break it to him.

He smiles a nostalgic smile. "Mom told me. I'm glad she reconnected with her family and found what she needed."

"Yeah, well, Braxton can be an ass sometimes, and he did steal my closest friend away from me, but he makes her happy, and Lily Claire is the cutest little baby girl."

"I bet she is," he murmurs.

"Oh, don't look so sad. If you guys had stayed together, she would have hated Boston. That girl is a full-blown redneck now. I'm talking *moonshine, cow patties, and riding around, slinging mud all over the place on purpose*, redneck. You'd have been miserable if you'd married her. She would have shown up to your company parties in overalls and boots and ruined your chance at ever making partner. You dodged a bullet, I'm telling you."

That causes him to laugh.

"Thank goodness," he agrees.

"Besides," I say as I lay my glass on the bar, "you have your new friend, who you obviously like very much. So, maybe that's the way it was supposed to happen."

He doesn't agree or disagree. He just sets his glass beside mine and extends his hand.

"Let your brother spin you around the dance floor for a while?" he asks.

"I thought you'd never ask."

We join our parents, who are cutting a rug together, and dance the night away.

Two

CHARLOTTE

I WAVE TO MY BROTHER, WHO'S SITTING IN THE BACK OF AN UBER, as I watch it drive away from the curb. He insisted on accompanying me back to my apartment before heading to his hotel room. Silly, I navigate the streets of New York on my own at night all the time, but I indulge him. It's not worth the argument. Mom had wanted him to stay with her and Dad while he was in town, but he opted for a room at The Plaza. Who could blame him?

I could use a spa and room service myself right about now.

He consoled her by promising to take us girls shopping and to lunch tomorrow while Dad golfs.

"Hi, George," I call to the doorman and wince as I stagger toward the entrance to my building. I've been wearing these gorgeous silver stiletto sling-backs since noon, and my feet are killing me.

"Charlotte, how was your evening?" George asks as he uses his key card to open the door for me.

I make it to him, and he takes my hand to help me in. I stop and balance myself in his grip as I proceed to remove my shoes.

Ah, that's so much better.

"It was exhausting. How about yours?"

"Same old," he answers as he waits for me to steady myself.

"I brought you some goodies," I tell him as I lift the bag wrapped around my right wrist, next to my clutch handle.

I loaded a bag down with all the leftover confections and a bottle of the expensive wine left after the party just for him. He's such a kind man, and I always feel safe, coming and going alone, with him at the door.

"Ah, thank you," he says.

I lift on my tiptoes and kiss his weathered cheek. "Happy New Year," I singsong.

"And a happy New Year to you too, Charlotte," he returns as he guides me into the lobby.

He waits until I am safely inside the elevator before taking his seat on the stool under the heat lamp out on the sidewalk again.

The elevator takes forever to climb to my floor. I'm so tired. I remember a time I could party the night straight through, drink all the cocktails, and end with a slice of pizza pie at Sal's at five in the morning before coming home to splash my face with water, reapply my lipstick, and make it to my morning class like a pro.

I walk into my apartment and drop the shoes next to the door as a ringing comes from my bag.

I glance at the clock on the microwave, and it's just past one in the morning.

I fish out the phone and see it's a video call from Sophie.

I accept the call, and the screen illuminates with my bestie's flushed face.

"Char! Happy New Year," she shouts at the screen.

"Happy New Year to you too—well, in an hour, right? It's eleven there?"

"Yep, I wanted to call you at midnight your time, but the baby was screaming," she says.

"Where are you?" I ask.

There is commotion in the background, and I can't make out the location.

"I'm at Dallas's house. We all decided to get together over here so that it would be easier for her with Beau and Faith. Braxton has been trying to keep Lily Claire awake, so he can kiss both his girls at midnight."

Dallas is Sophie's childhood best friend. They reconnected when she returned to Poplar Falls and their friendship picked back up like she never left. Dallas married Myer Wilson a couple years ago and he adopted her son, Beau, from a previous marriage before they welcomed their baby girl, Faith, a couple months before Sophie gave birth to her and Braxton's daughter, Lily Claire.

"Where is she? Auntie Char wants to say hi."

"She and Faith are both in Faith's crib. She just couldn't hold on any longer," she says before a boom goes off. The screen jerks, and she goes out of the frame.

"Hawk! Come here, buddy," she calls out.

"What is happening?" I ask.

"Sorry," she says as she comes back on the screen. "Walker's drunk ass has been shooting off fireworks for the last hour, and the dogs are going nuts."

Walker is Braxton's best friend. He works on Sophie's family's ranch and is engaged to Braxton's baby sister, Elle.

"You brought Hawkeye to the New Year's Eve party?"

"Yes. Braxton didn't want to leave him at home alone. He's been clingy since he lost his sight in his one eye and the baby came. So, we brought him along. Then, when Walker and Elle showed up, Walker got all up in arms because Cowboy and Hawk were having a playdate, and Woof wasn't invited, so he went back and got him," she explains.

Hawkeye is Braxton's bulldog who lost an eye protecting a

pregnant Sophie from a rattlesnake. That dog protects both Sophie and Lily Claire with his life.

"So, you are at a New Year's party with two babies, an eight-year-old, and three dogs?" I ask.

"I sure am," she says as she giggles.

Her attention goes to the side of the screen, and she talks to Beau, off camera.

Then, his face appears, and he grins at me.

"Hey, Miss Charlotte," he shouts above the dogs' barking.

"Hey, buddy. Where did your teeth go?" I ask him.

He gifts me with a wide, gap-toothed grin.

"They got loose, and Daddy pulled them. The tooth fairy left me ten dollars," he says excitedly.

"Ten dollars? Wow, I know who's taking me out to dinner the next time I'm in town, rich man," I tease.

He nods his agreement and then passes the phone off to his uncle Payne.

"Hey there, hot stuff," he says with a sexy smile.

"Hey, you," I say as I crawl up on my bed, still in my dress.

"Did you have a good night?" he asks.

"Not as good as it would have been if you were here to help get me out of this dress," I say as I angle the camera down my body so he can see all of me.

He chuckles, and the sound pours over me like warm honey.

"Damn. I tried to get you to stay until after the first," he reminds me.

"I know, but I promised my mother I'd be back for tonight."

Regret fills me. I should have stayed. I'd love nothing more than to be sitting out there with all of them, watching fireworks fill the starry sky.

"Maybe next year," he says before a loud bang, and then lights go streaking by his head in rapid succession.

I hear Dallas's voice screaming from somewhere behind Payne, "Walker Reid, you drunk asshole. If you hurt my son or catch my house on fire, I will come out there and shove one of those rockets where the sun don't shine."

"Sorry, Dal. It was Braxton's fault. He didn't set it up correctly," I hear Walker's voice yell from somewhere in the distance.

"Oh shit, I gotta go, hon. I have to go get control of Walker before Dallas attacks him. I'll call you later," he says as he hurriedly passes the phone back to Sophie.

She fumbles to get control of it, and the phone falls to the ground. When she picks it up, it skims the yard upside down, and I see Walker standing over a bottle that has fallen over with sizzling sticks hanging out of it. Payne has made it close to him, and he stops and spreads his arms out to block a female I do not recognize from the explosive. She clings to his back with her face buried into his shirt as Braxton dives for the bottle and turns it the opposite direction a second before it goes off.

The screen swings up as the sky illuminates, and then Sophie's face is back.

"Braxton is going to kill Walker," she whispers at me.

"Who is the blonde?" I ask as jealousy slithers down my spine.

"Huh?" she asks, confused.

"The blonde. I saw a blonde I don't know out in the yard."

She looks up and narrows her eyes as she scans the people.

"Oh, you mean Katlynn. She's Foster's cousin, I believe," she says.

"Oh."

"I have to go, Char. I think that last blast woke the babies up. I hope you have a good rest of your night. We miss you. Happy New Year!"

I don't even get *I miss you guys too* out before the screen goes black and silent.

I roll over and place the phone in the charger on my nightstand, and then I stare up at my ceiling.

Five weeks. Five long weeks before I head back to Colorado for Elle and Walker's wedding. I know it will fly by with all the work I have to do.

Sophia Doreen Designs was slammed with orders during the holidays. This past quarter was our most profitable yet. It's exciting, and I wish Sophie were here to celebrate with me. Don't get me wrong; I'm happy for her. Braxton is amazing, and that baby girl is just everything, but I miss having her here in the city with me.

Katlynn. Foster's cousin.

I wonder why I've never heard of her before. I'm sure there are lots of women in Poplar Falls that I have yet to meet. It's not a big deal.

I look over to the clock and see it's five minutes until two. That means, they are starting the New Year's countdown at Dallas's. I wonder if Katlynn brought a date to kiss or if her lips will be seeking a partner.

Ugh.

I grab the pillow from beside me, hold it over my face, and scream into it.

That felt good.

I don't know if I'm more annoyed by Katlynn or the fact that I am annoyed by Katlynn. I'm not that girl. Never have been.

My phone dings.

I sit up and grab it from its nest and read the text from Payne.

Payne: *Leave that sexy dress on until I get home and call you. I want to watch as you peel it off.*

That sends an altogether different sensation tingling down my spine.

Ha! Take that, Katlynn.

Me: You got it, cowboy.

I hit Send on my response and lie back down, willing myself to stay awake a little longer.

Three

Charlotte: *You're the devil. Spin class was miserable this morning, and it's all your fault.*

I read the text from Charlotte as I climb into my truck to meet the guys.

Today, we're starting the work to get the chapel ready for Walker and Elle's wedding day.

I pull up the photo she sent me of her in the shimmering, low-cut, long-sleeved silver dress, the hem hitting just above her exposed knee. It hugged her curves in just the right way, and the memory of watching her slowly peel it down the length of her body causes an uncomfortable tightness in my jeans.

Me: *I'm not the least bit sorry.*

I type the reply and hit Send as I remember our video call from last night. She was a sleepy, sexy sight in that tiny sequined dress.

I never understood the appeal of phone sex before. It always seemed cold and impersonal to me. I imagined some sleazy hermit in his parents' basement, getting himself off to a sultry stranger's voice on the other end of the line, who was charging him by the minute for his pleasure.

I prefer a warm body underneath me, and I like to feel a woman's breath on my neck as she screams my name when she comes, but somehow, Charlotte has made long-distance teasing into an art form, and my body is very much on board with our improvised nights together.

I pull into the drive in front of Myer and Dallas's house and lay on my horn. The yard is still a mess with the remnants of our celebration from last night. I probably need to help Myer with cleanup when we get back.

He emerges a few minutes later and climbs into the passenger seat, looking worse for wear.

I don't know how Walker convinced us to start this project on New Year's Day, but here we are.

It's about a ten-mile drive out to the old chapel on the outskirts of Poplar Falls, and by the time we arrive, Walker, Braxton, and Silas, one of the full-time employees at Rustic Peak Ranch, are already hauling equipment off the back of Braxton's truck and into the open front doors.

I pull in and park next to them.

"Morning," I greet as I hop down and slam the door shut.

"Jeez, do you have to yell?" Walker grumbles as he passes, carrying a drop cloth and toolbox.

"What's wrong with him?" I ask Braxton as I walk over and take one end of the generator he is sliding toward the tailgate.

"Hangover." It's all the explanation he gives as we lift the machine up and carry it into the chapel.

This is the place that Braxton and Elle's mother and father were married. The church that owns it moved a few years back, and the chapel fell into disrepair as it sat, waiting to be demolished to make room for a new community playground for the neighborhood children. Elle had her heart set on getting married here, and with a little finesse, Walker was able to convince the church board to let us fix the place up for her big day and then convert the building into a recreation room for the kids.

He recruited us for free labor, and it's a win-win for both the happy couple and the children of the community, so none of us mind.

The only catch is that it needs to be completed within the next couple weeks in order to be ready for the wedding set for Valentine's weekend.

Thank goodness January is a slow month for both ranchers and us in the farming industry. Hopefully, we have enough hands and plenty of spare time to get the job done for our friends.

We work steadily until noon and then take a break for lunch. Doreen and Ria, Braxton's aunts, sent a cooler packed down with sandwiches, chips, and water.

"Whose idea was it to start this project the day after celebrating New Year's Eve?" Walker asks.

"Yours, asshat," Braxton answers as he tosses a chip at him.

"Oh, right," Walker mumbles.

"I'll expect you at my house after dinner too. You have a bunch of fireworks scraps and bottles to pick up before Dallas comes looking for you," Myer tells him.

"Dal's gotten uptight since you two got married. She used to be the one out there, holding the bottle for me."

"You were aiming rockets at her house with her children inside." Myer takes up for his wife.

"Not intentionally. Braxton sucks as a spotter. It was his fault they kept tipping over and firing in that direction."

"Your drunk ass was knocking them over as soon as I could get them set up," Braxton defends.

"Next year, the party is going to be at my house, so no one will bitch about the quality of the fireworks display," Walker retorts.

"Do you think Elle is going to be the one female in history who doesn't care if her drunk husband and his idiot friends burn her home to the ground?" I ask him.

"She's marrying me. She has to be tough," he says on a shrug.

We all nod in agreement because it's the truth. The girl is signing up for a lifetime of dumbassery.

We finish eating and make our way back inside to get a couple of more hours of work done before heading home for the traditional New Year's dinner of hog jowls, black-eyed peas, and collard greens with our families. The old wives' tale is that if you consume those items on January 1, your year will be blessed with eating high on the hog, good luck, and a financial windfall. I've been forcing it down since I was a kid and never felt any booster in luck or fortune. My granddad told me it only works for you once in your lifetime, but you don't want to miss a year because it could be your year. Therefore, I continue to choke it down every damn New Year's Day, just in case he was right.

"Speaking of last night, Foster said Katlynn was asking after you this morning, Payne. He wasn't sure what to tell her," Myer says.

"Yeah, she gave me her phone number last night. Told me to call her sometime."

I continue to pull up flooring as Walker chimes in, "Are you going to ask her out?"

I look up at him and shrug. "Probably not. I'm not looking for any kind of entanglement, and the last thing I should be doing is getting involved with a friend's relative."

His eyes slice to me, and a look of confusion creases his brow. "Any entanglement?"

"That's right," I insist.

"I'm pretty sure he has all the entanglement he can handle right now with a feisty little blonde New Yorker," Myer interjects.

"Dude, Braxton is right there," Walker whisper-shouts to him as he gestures over his shoulder.

"What?" Myer asks, confused.

Walker looks at me. "I know Sophie is hot and all, but it's not cool to be talking about her while her husband is in the building."

I pick up the closest piece of discarded floorboard and chuck it at him. "He means Charlotte, you jackass," I say as the wood plunks him in the side.

"Hey, we're in the Lord's house. You shouldn't be cursing, asshole," he retorts.

"What is the status of your relationship with Charlotte anyway?" Myer asks.

I look up and see three expectant faces watching me. "What are we now, women? Are we going to talk about our feelings and shit?" I ask them.

"It's okay, buddy. You're in the circle of trust. This is a safe place," Walker says as he lays his hand on my back.

I give him a searing look, and he throws both his hands in the air and backs away.

"Okay, looks like we've hit a nerve," he continues.

"The truth is, I have no idea what our status is. I like her. She likes me. We enjoy each other's company when she's in town. That's about all I know."

Myer nods.

"It sounds solid to me," Braxton defends.

"Solid? It sounds as fragile as a butterfly's wing to me," Walker adds.

"Butterfly's wing?" Braxton repeats. "We *are* turning into women."

"I'm comfortable enough in my manhood to show my sensitive side," Walker claims, and then he points at me. "As for you, that's how it starts. A woman gets under your skin, and the next thing you know, you're disinterested in every other woman who throws herself at you. Then, you find yourself going home at night instead of to the bar, and you begin dressing nicer and keeping your house cleaner. Then, wham! Before you know it, you're caught in the trap," he says.

"What trap?"

"The trap every single one of us has fallen into. The love and marriage trap."

"I wouldn't let Elle hear you call it a trap if I were you," Braxton advises.

"I never said she was the one doing the trapping." He grins at his soon-to-be brother-in-law.

Four

CHARLOTTE

I SHOWER AT THE GYM AND DRESS QUICKLY. I PULL ON AN OVERSIZE emerald-green cable-knit sweater, black leggings, and a pair of green patent leather booties. I swipe on some lip gloss and leave my hair loose. It's growing out from the pixie cut I wore the past few years. It hits just below my shoulders now, and I enjoy being able to pull it up in a topknot or in a low ponytail again.

My phone dings just as I throw my bag back into my locker and spin the combination lock. It's Alex, letting me know that he, Mom, and Mila are around the corner and should be here in five minutes.

I make my way to the entrance and stand out on the curb to await their car.

A black SUV pulls up at the light, and when the back door slides open, my family steps out.

Mila has on a baby-pink crushed velvet Gucci track suit with a crop top, and her dark hair is piled on top of her head. She is sporting a clean face and dark sunglasses. Mom looks perfectly coiffed in her silk blouse and knee-length skirt, and Alex is casually dressed in a henley and jeans.

"Hi, sis. Are you hungry?" Alex asks as they make it to me.

I shrug. "I could eat," I answer.

"How about brunch at Lilith's?" he suggests.

I look down at my phone to see the time is just shy of noon.

"We can try to get in, but it'll be a long shot without reservations," I tell him.

"I've got it covered," he says as he wraps his arm around my neck and guides the three of us across the street in the direction of one of his favorite spots in the city.

"So, what's on the agenda for today?" I ask as we weave our way through the lunchtime sidewalk crowd.

"Eating and shopping—my girls' favorite pastimes," Alex informs me.

We take a left at the next city block and run right into a line that is at least thirty bodies deep.

"I knew it. The wait is going to be forever," I say as my stomach grumbles in protest as soon as the aroma of waffles and bacon hits my nose.

Alex marches us past all the waiting patrons and into a side door that leads to the hostess.

"Name?" she asks as we approach her podium.

"Alex Claiborne, party of five."

She looks down at her tablet and smiles. "Yes, sir. Your other guest has already arrived. Please, follow me," she says as she grabs menus and leads us to a table tucked into a cozy corner.

Blake Thornton stands as he catches sight of us.

Great.

"Blake," Alex greets as he gives Blake a fist bump. "Thanks for getting us in, man. I appreciate it."

"Blake, how lovely to see you," Mom says as she tilts her head for him to kiss her cheek before sliding in beside him.

"Mila, Charlotte, beautiful as always, ladies," he says as we all take our seats.

"You look awfully chipper today," Mila says to Blake as she

pours herself a large cup of black coffee from the carafe sitting on the table.

He ignores her comment as he waves the server over to take our drink orders.

We chat as a round of mimosas and a couple Bloody Marys are brought out.

"Charlotte, would you like to split a stack of blueberry pancakes with me?" Blake asks.

I cut my eyes to him. "No, thank you," I say sweetly.

"You're still miffed at me, I see," he says as he looks over his menu.

"Whatever for?" Mom asks.

"Nothing of importance. It's just a misunderstanding," Blake tells her.

"Hardly," I protest. "You insulted Payne."

"Payne? What's that?" Alex asks.

"Apparently, it's a name," Blake scoffs.

I toss my menu and prop my elbows on the table as I glare at him. "Don't make me be mean to you again," I dare him.

"Charlotte, keep your voice down, for goodness' sake," Mom scolds.

I sit up straight and mumble a quick, "Sorry."

"Who is this Payne you two are rowing over?" Alex asks.

"Charlotte's hot country fling," Mila offers.

Alex's eyes come to me, and he raises his brows.

"He is a friend from Poplar Falls. He was visiting me over the Christmas holiday, and I made the mistake of taking him to meet some of my friends here in New York for drinks and dinner. I didn't expect them to treat him like he was the dirt beneath their fingernails."

"It wasn't that bad," Blake defends, "and we said nothing

insulting to his face. Charlotte overheard comments, and she took them out of context."

"Sure I did." I scowl at him.

"Honestly, Charlotte, the man looked like he belonged on a tractor somewhere, not having cocktails at the Warwick. What did you expect would happen?" Blake asks.

"I thought he was hot," Mila interrupts.

Blake cuts his eyes to her and scowls.

"You're such a snob," she retorts.

"Children, let's not name-call. We're here to enjoy a nice afternoon together. Alex, why don't you tell us about your new apartment?" Mom tries to steer the conversation into a more civilized direction.

"So, you and this Payne guy are an item?" Alex asks, refusing to let it go.

I shrug. "We're something," I give my non-answer.

"Well, that certainly clears it up," he states.

"What kind of name is Payne anyway?" Blake is like a dog with a bone.

"A rugged one," I reply.

"Rugged? Really, Charlotte? A name can be rugged?" he asks.

"It sure can, Blakey Poo," I say as I bat my eyelashes at him.

Mila snort-laughs.

Mom sighs.

"Can we talk about something else, please?" she asks, and I give her a grateful smile.

Blake joins us for our day of shopping, much to my dismay.

"He still has it bad for you," Mila says as we follow him, Alex, and Mom toward Fifth Avenue.

"No, he doesn't. He's just being a brat," I tell her.

"No, it's so obvious. He's jealous."

Pot, meet kettle. I can see the jealousy humming under the surface of her passive facade.

When we were in high school, I was infatuated with Blake. He was my older brother's attractive best friend. I thought he was cool, and he treated Sophie and me like he enjoyed having us around—unlike Alex, who wanted nothing to do with us. That was, until he fell head over heels for Sophie years later.

I used to go to great lengths to get and keep Blake's attention.

We finally hooked up after college and began casually dating but the infatuation quickly fizzled. At least it did for me. I realized that the man I had built him up to be in my imagination was a far cry from the boring frat boy he actually was.

Now, it seems he has caught the attention of my baby sister.

"Trust me, Mila, I have zero interest in Blake Thornton. That ship sailed a long time ago," I tell her.

"I'm not so sure he realizes that," she mutters under her breath.

I decide it's time for a little sisterly advice, so I slow my pace as the guys and our mother walk ahead of us.

Mila looks at me in confusion as I tug the hem of her top.

"Blake is the type of man who wants what he can't have," I point out.

She shrugs like it doesn't matter to her. "Obviously."

"He's arrogant and proud of himself, but he's also handsome, loyal, and successful. The right woman could tame him," I continue.

"Why would I care?" she asks.

I give her a knowing look. Then, I wrap my arm around her

neck and pull her in close. "Just listen to your older and wiser sister for once. Blake likes the chase. So, if you want to get his attention, you have to start the game of cat and mouse," I begin.

She keeps her eyes forward, but I can tell by her body language that she is listening intently.

"The trick is to let him believe he is the cat."

At that, her eyes slide to mine, and she smiles a cunning smile.

"I can do that," she whispers.

"Oh, I have no doubt that you can," I say as I release her, and we catch up with Mom and the boys.

Alex and Blake pop into a corner bar for a drink while we girls peruse the wares in one of Fifth Avenue's trendy boutiques. Mila and Mom sit on the velvet bench at the end of the aisle of gorgeous stilettos as an overly helpful sales associate brings box after box of heels for them to try on.

"Can I bring something out for you, miss?" he asks me as I glance at the beautiful red-soled offerings.

"I'm just looking for now. Thank you," I reply when a pair of handsome tan-and-tobacco knee-high boots catch my eye. "Oh," I say. "Do you have those in a six and a half?" I ask as I point them out.

"I'll check in the back," he says before he scurries off.

Mila looks at me in the mirror. "I thought you were shopping for shoes to match your new dress?" she asks.

I walk over and sit on the bench across from them. "I am. I think those would look amazing with the simple cotton dress I bought to wear to Walker and Elle's wedding."

My mother's mouth drops open. "Riding boots? You're going to wear riding boots to a wedding?" she asks in horror.

The sales associate returns with a box and hands me one boot to try on.

I slide it on and zip it up the side as I answer, "Nine-hundred-dollar Ralph Lauren riding boots."

"But it's a wedding," she pushes.

"Yeah, well, if you knew the groom, you wouldn't be so shocked. I wouldn't put it past him to show up in a flannel suit," I say on a laugh.

The appalled look that both my sister and mother are giving me is comical. I'm sure they could never imagine attending such a laid-back affair.

"You're kidding, right?" Mom asks.

I shrug. "Sort of. I mean, he could honestly show up in cowboy boots and jeans, but Elle wouldn't mind. She'll look like a princess in her mother's wedding gown. They love each other madly, and that's all that matters."

Mila gives Mom a look that screams, *Sure it is.*

"Charlotte, sweetheart, I'm starting to worry about you spending so much time in Colorado."

"Oh, Mom, don't worry. I won't corrupt them—too much," I tell her.

Five

CHARLOTTE

I FINISH UP MY TELECONFERENCE WITH THE NEW MARKETING FIRM that is taking over the reins of our spring collection. The new nationwide campaign will be featured in every zip code and stars one of Hollywood's up-and-coming A-listers.

I have just enough time to run back to my condo and pick up my bags before I stop for my meeting in the Diamond District.

We are launching our first ever engagement ring collection, and Sophie wants to hand-pick the supplier of our stones. I'm doing all the preliminary vetting so that when she comes into town for our fiscal year-end in March, everything will be ready for us to choose the company we want to work with exclusively, and contracts can be finalized.

Then, I'll leave straight for the airport to head to Poplar Falls for over three weeks of wedding and Valentine's Day festivities.

Sophie and I will fly to San Diego for a meeting with a West Coast distributor at the end of the month, and then I will come home the first week of March.

"Are you moving, Charlotte?" George asks as I exit the elevator with my loaded-down luggage cart

I look at the pile and sigh. "No, I'm just going to be gone for a month," I assure him.

"An entire month this time?"

"Yeah, I know. It seems like I'm away more than I'm home, doesn't it?" I ask just as the black sedan pulls up to the curb.

"It sure does. It makes for an exciting life, I bet. I'll make sure the front desk holds your mail until you return. Safe travels," George says as he holds the door for the driver who comes to help me with my things.

"Thank you, George. Have a happy Valentine's Day," I say as I climb in the backseat.

I'm excited to be heading back to Sophie and Lily Claire—and Payne. It's only been a little over a month since I saw them, but it feels like ages.

It's funny how my time in Poplar Falls seems to fly by, but when I'm home and waiting to go back, it halts to a slow crawl.

The driver drops me off for my appointment but waits around the corner for my meeting to be over. It's short and sweet.

Then, it's straight to the airport.

Seated next to me on my flight is a very handsome and very chatty silver fox. A gentleman named Robert. He is a venture capitalist from the city, and we spend the entire two-hour flight discussing what brings the both of us to Colorado.

He is looking to invest in a new gaming company that is headquartered in Denver.

I tell him all about Sophia Doreen Designs—from our conception in the floor of Sophie's and my shared college apartment to the explosion that happened right before Sophie moved from the city to where we are today.

"That's an incredible story. Very few companies under five years old see that level of growth in such a short period of time," he praises.

"Thank you. We've both worked extremely hard, and it's paying off," I say, pride clear in my reply.

"We should get dinner sometime when we're both back in the city. I'd love to hear more about the direction you're headed," he says as he reaches into his wallet and pulls out a business card.

I take it from his hand. "Robert James Investments," I read the bold print aloud. "I'll give you a call sometime," I promise as the flight attendant announces we are preparing for landing.

We say our good-byes as we deplane, and when I arrive at Baggage Claim, Sophie is standing at the bottom of the escalator with Lily Claire in a sling tied around her neck. She's holding a handmade sign that says, World's Best Auntie.

I squeal when I catch sight of them and practically bowl over an older couple to get to them.

"How was your flight?" Sophie asks as she follows me to the carousel.

"Bumpy," I say as I look around for Braxton. "Where's Braxton?"

"He was busy at the ranch, so the baby and I drove up ourselves," she informs me.

Oh no.

"Soph, I have, like, a hundred bags. How are we going to get them out to your car?"

"A hundred?" Her eyes grow round in disbelief.

"Close to it. I'm here for almost four weeks, and I need wedding clothes, snow clothes, business clothes ... all the clothes. And shoes," I exclaim.

"You're going to have to leave some things here in Colorado.

You can fill one of the spare closets at my house, or you can leave stuff at Payne's cabin. It's getting ridiculous, you carting everything back and forth every few weeks," she says as I pluck my bags one by one from the conveyor belt.

"Payne doesn't want me leaving all my girlie things at his house. It will look like he's a taken man," I tell her.

I turn and wave down an airport employee to ask if they have any available luggage carts. He just grunts at me and keeps walking.

"Very helpful! Thank you!" I shout after him.

"He kind of is a taken man, don't you think?" Sophie asks.

"What?" I bring my attention back to her.

"Payne. He kind of is taken, right? I mean, you stay with him every time you're in Poplar Falls, and you're in Poplar Falls at least as much as you're in New York these days. You two practically live together."

My mouth drops open as she finishes.

She shrugs.

"I don't think he would see it that way," I tell her.

"If you say so."

"Stay here and watch these bags, and I'll go chase down a cart," I instruct, and she sits on the edge of my mountain of cargo to guard it while I go in search of help.

I walk up and down the Baggage Claim area and don't find a single empty cart, so I venture out of the sliding glass doors to the car pickup line.

The Arrivals area is slammed today. The car line is bumper-to-bumper, and exhausted, grumpy commuters are rushing around with their bags in tow. Horns are honking, and taxi drivers are cursing each other. I'm about to give up the search when I spot a man with a cart, loading the trunk of a Mercedes, and approach him.

"Excuse me. Are you finished with that cart?" I ask.

"I am." He turns and smiles, and it's none other than Robert James. "We meet again, Charlotte. It's serendipitous," he says with a smile. Then, he passes the empty cart over to me.

"Thank you."

"I didn't get your number," he says as I turn to go back inside.

"What was that?"

"Your contact information. In case you lose mine. I really would like to see you again," he says.

"Oh, I left my purse inside with my friend. My business cards are in it."

"One sec," he says as he holds up a finger.

He walks around to the driver's side of the Mercedes and speaks to the person behind the wheel. The car drives off, and he returns to me and takes the cart from my grip.

"What are you doing?" I ask.

"I told my friend to circle the airport twice. I'll help you get your things, and you can give me your number," he says. "Deal?"

"Deal," I agree.

We make our way back to Sophie and the baby.

"You found one," she says as we approach. "Thank goodness."

"Yep, and some muscle to go along with it. Sophie, this is Robert James. Robert, this is Sophia Lancaster," I introduce.

Sophie extends her hand to him. "It's Young actually. Sophia Young, but you can call me Sophie."

"Crap. I keep forgetting your married name," I say in apology.

"It's fine. I catch myself doing it sometimes too."

"Ah, the artist of the company," Robert surmises.

Sophie looks confused.

"Robert was my seatmate on the flight. We talked all about our respective businesses. He even knows Stanhope," I fill her in.

Stanhope Marshall is married to Sophie's mother, Vivian. He is a prominent New York business executive and is known and respected by many.

"Yes, Stanhope and I have had the pleasure of working together in the past. He's a good man."

"He's the best," Sophie agrees.

"Are those the bags I'm here to help get to your vehicle, so you guys can be off to Poplar Falls?" Robert asks her.

"Yes, thank you," Sophie says as she stands to allow Robert to load up my bags and help us out to the truck.

Once he has everything in the back of the pickup, I fish one of my cards from my purse and hand it to him.

"It was nice to meet you again, Robert James," I tell him as he takes the card and slips it into his breast pocket.

"Likewise, Charlotte Claiborne, and you too, Sophie," he says with a smile. "You'll be hearing from me soon."

He takes the cart and rolls it back toward the airport.

Sophie gets the baby strapped in, and we are on our way.

"That was interesting," she muses as we pull out of the parking deck.

"What was?" I ask.

"Mr. Robert James. He was quite smitten with you," she points out.

I shrug. "He was nice and smart. I figure he's a good contact for us to have. Networking is part of the job."

"Uh-huh, if you say so."

"He's probably old enough to be my father," I point out.

"Like that matters."

She's right. At our age it's no big deal, but I'm honestly not interested in anything beyond a business connection.

Six

PAYNE

Charlotte: *I just landed. See you soon, cowboy.*

I read the text from Charlotte as I load my truck with the supplies I need for the day's work and smile.

It's been a minute since she was here last, and I have a few Valentine's Day surprises up my sleeve for her.

The trick will be to keep her out of the spare bedroom for the next week and a half. I threw an old horse blanket over the gift I stashed in there and added a couple of smelly shirts and a pair of worn-out jeans for good measure, hoping it would deter her from investigating.

If I close the door and lock it, she'll get curious—or more like suspicious—and then she'll try her best to figure out why I want to keep her out of there.

Maybe I should go that route just to get her riled up.

I laugh to myself as I picture her with a hairpin, trying to pick the lock while I'm out working. The woman has no shame, and it's one of the things I love about her.

Love?

The guys have gotten into my head ever since our conversation at the chapel. I've never given much thought to where Charlotte and I stand before. The truth is, when this whole thing started, I did not know how intricately she would be woven into our lives here in Poplar Falls. She was just the quirky, sexy-as-hell little spitfire from the city who was visiting Sophie. I don't think either of us expected anything beyond a fun one-night stand on the first night we spent together in that tent. When she left at the end of the week, I wasn't sure I'd ever see her again.

That seems like a lifetime ago. Now, she's as much a part of my day as anyone else. I wake up, thinking about her, and text her good morning every single day. Most nights, she's the last thing I think about and the last voice I hear.

I even surprised her by showing up in New York City last month. Surprised myself too, if I'm being honest. It was my first trip to Manhattan. I never had a reason to go there before, but I wanted to see her. I missed her. The trip didn't go as planned, and we ended up on a plane back to Poplar Falls two days later.

Something shifted in our relationship over the holidays. I can't quite put my finger on what that means for us, but it's definitely there. A question lingering in the air between us as I dropped her off at the airport the weekend after Christmas.

I guess we should talk about that soon, but I've never been the *let's define our relationship* type of person before, and I get the impression that neither has she.

I spend the afternoon out in the orchard, prepping it for the hard freeze that is being forecasted for the next couple of weeks. The days are shorter and colder, so there are limited work hours this time of year.

I'm sealing a tree when I feel a vibration against my hip.

I lay down my brush and fish my phone out of my back pocket to see Charlotte's name illuminating the screen.

"Hey, sweetheart," I greet.

"Hey, sexy. What are you doing?" she asks, her voice playful.

"Painting trees," I answer.

"What?" she asks.

"Painting apple trees. What are you doing?" I ask.

"I thought I heard you correctly. Why would you paint apple trees?" she asks, confusion in her voice.

"We have to paint the trunks of the trees in the orchard with white latex paint every January. It reflects light and protects them from sunscald coming off the snow. It also protects the bark from splitting and cracking as they thaw from a freeze," I explain.

"Oh, so you are literally painting the trees. Thank goodness. For a second, I thought you were going all soft and artsy on me and were sitting in a meadow somewhere with an easel and oil paints," she says on a laugh.

"Hey, there's nothing soft about being artsy," I hear Sophie's offended response in the background.

"Oops," Charlotte whispers into the phone and then giggles. "How long are you going to be out there?" she asks.

"A couple more hours on this side of the orchard. The rest can wait until tomorrow. Where are you?" I ask.

"I'm at Sophie and Braxton's house."

"Are you planning on staying there or with me?"

"Well, I could pretend that I'm planning to stay here, but then we both know you'll just have to bring me over to dig through my stuff every other day, and when it's time to go home, I'll have half my stuff here and half my stuff at your house, and packing will be a nightmare," she rambles.

"So, let's make this easy on everyone, and I'll come pick you and all your shit up when I get done here," I interrupt.

"Oh, all right, if you insist." She fakes exasperation.

I chuckle. "It'll be late. I need to finish up and run home to shower."

"That's fine. I need my baby snuggle time anyway," she agrees. "Just text me when you are on your way, and I'll be ready," she starts and then pauses. "Hold on a sec, Payne."

I hear a mumbled conversation, and then she comes back on the line.

"Sophie is going to make chili and cornbread for dinner. Are you hungry? Do you want to eat here with her and Braxton when you're done with work?" she asks.

My stomach rumbles at the mention of food. "Chili sounds amazing."

"Then, it's a date," she says.

"In that case, I'll try to make it over sooner. Can I bring anything?" I ask.

"No. Just you," she says.

"Give me two hours, and I'll be there."

"Okay, bye."

She disconnects, and I decide to call it a day. The trees will be here tomorrow, and I can't wait to see my girl.

I load everything into the back of my pickup and head home to freshen up.

Seven

CHARLOTTE

SOPHIE AND I SPEND THE EVENING TALKING BUSINESS AS I ASSIST her in the kitchen.

I'm not much of a cook. Honestly, I don't think I've ever even turned on the oven in my condo, except maybe to reheat a slice of pizza or chicken wings. Why bother cooking for one when you can get delivery or takeout and not have to deal with the cleanup?

Sophie wasn't much better before she moved back to Poplar Falls, but her aunts, Doreen and Ria, are the best damn cooks on the planet and have taken her under their wings, and she's gotten quite good.

I chop an onion into cubes, as instructed, while she pulls a variety of spices from the cabinet above the coffeemaker.

"So, you think we should go with Goldstein for diamonds?" she asks over her shoulder.

"Goldstein or Moses, for sure. I lined up meetings with both for your visit in March, so you can decide between them. I did a lot of research, read a ton of reviews, and actually interviewed a couple of jewelers in the city, and both are highly recommended. Their diamonds are high quality, their prices are competitive, they deliver on time, and best of all, they both want to work with Sophia Doreen Designs," I explain.

"Hmm, sounds like you've got all of our bases covered. I wonder if Stanhope knows either of them personally," she says.

"Your mother is a fan of Goldstein. She's the one who sent me his contact information. Apparently, a few of her diamonds were resourced from him."

"She has excellent taste in jewels. Have you heard any updates on when they plan to start the manufacturing expansion?" She changes the subject.

"No, we're still waiting to get through all the red tape with the city," I tell her.

"Dammit, I was hoping that would be finished by this summer. We are burning through our budget, sourcing out the work," she complains.

"I know. And the lease for the additional space is triple what we are paying for our current warehouse. I wish we could just move the entire operation out of Manhattan," I grumble.

She turns and props a hip against the counter. "Maybe we should look into that."

I stop my chopping and glance up at her. "It'd be expensive. We'd have to location scout, move equipment, relocate staff or hire new staff, and we're already behind on our timeline," I point out.

"Okay, hear me out. What if we launch the engagement line next year instead of this year? If we found somewhere that had more space for less money, a place we could purchase instead of leasing, it would pay off in the long run. The only reason we are where we are now is because it was so close to our office and my condo in the city, and I was still literally crafting most of the pieces myself back then. It was convenient, and we didn't know what we were doing."

I scrape the pile of cubed onions from the cutting board into the hot frying pan. "I guess that's true. I can start looking at places.

But you must break the news to Maple and Park if we push back the engagement line. I don't think it will go over well."

Maple and Park is a fine department store in New York City that carries an exclusive line of Sophia Doreen Designs in their locations.

"I can handle them," she assures me. "Let's find out if there are any properties we are interested in first."

"Are you thinking Queens or Brooklyn?" I ask.

"Sure, or Jersey. Somewhere large enough for manufacturing and inventory. It would need office space and a shipping and handling department too."

I blow out a breath. "I can give Blake a call. He handles corporate real estate deals for his dad's firm on the side. He might have some leads for us if you're serious," I suggest.

"Yeah, let's explore our options. I mean, the city has us in limbo at the moment anyway."

"Okay. I'll call him in the morning. Look at us, tag-teaming dinner and hammering out strategic business moves. We are a dream team," I say just as smoke pours from the stove. "Shit, the onions," I cry.

Sophie grabs the handle of the pan and runs it to the sink. She turns on the water just as the fire alarm howls. Lily Claire's frightened cries come from the monitor, and I run to her nursery to comfort her.

When I walk back into the kitchen with the baby in my arms, Sophie is standing on a chair, fanning the smoke detector with a pot holder.

"Maybe we should wait until after dinner to talk shop next time, wonder twin," she grumbles.

With a brand-new cubed onion, some diced tomatoes, extra cayenne pepper, garlic powder, tomato paste, ground beef, kidney beans, coupled with our full attention, we are able to salvage dinner. Sophie is just pulling the cornbread muffins from the oven.

Payne texted about twenty minutes ago, saying he is on his way.

A thrill shoots through me when I hear his truck pull up outside. It's strange that I can distinguish the difference between the sound his truck makes versus the sound of Braxton's.

When did I develop that superpower?

I meet him at the back door, and I leap into his arms and start kissing his face. Thankfully, he catches me despite my unannounced assault.

"Did you miss me?" I ask as he carries me into the house.

"I did," he answers against my lips.

"I missed you too."

"I can't tell," he teases as he sets me on my feet.

"Hmm, I guess I'll just have to convince you later, then."

I watch as heat dances in his stormy eyes.

"Careful, or we'll be skipping dinner," he threatens.

The door opens behind him, and Braxton walks in.

"Hey, man," he greets Payne and then me, "Charlotte."

Sophie walks in from the living room, carrying a fussy Lily Claire. Apparently, someone didn't get her nap before being awakened by our loud cooking incident. She gives Braxton a quick kiss and hands their daughter off to her daddy.

He gently rocks her and talks softly to her about his day. Her tears dry, and she settles instantly, completely fascinated with every word coming from his mouth.

I look at Sophie, and she shakes her head.

"Every single time," she says. "When she hears his voice, she just calms. It's maddening."

"Don't worry. Before you know it, she'll be a teenager, and the sound of his voice will cause her eyes to roll so far back in her head that she'll be able to see her own thoughts," Payne tells her.

"How would you know?" I ask him.

He looks at me and grins. "I have a sister. Dallas went from the sweetest little girl in the world to an ornery teen overnight. Everything Dad or I had to say was stupid, and we could never understand what it was like to be a woman," he explains, bringing the back of his wrist to his forehead in a dramatic fashion.

"Jeez, don't rush her," Braxton mutters.

Payne slaps him on the back. "Time will do that all on its own, brother. Soak it all in while you can."

Lily Claire chooses that exact moment to let out a peal of giggles.

Payne looks down at her and runs his finger across her chin. "Yep, you've got his number, don't ya, little one?"

She blows a raspberry at him, and he chuckles.

He peers down at her with an indulgent smile. "I have that effect on women," he coos at her.

It looks to me like she has her uncle Payne's number too.

Eight

CHARLOTTE

AFTER DINNER, WE LOAD MY BELONGINGS INTO PAYNE'S TRUCK and head to his cabin on the outskirts of town. It's about ten miles from Sophie's home. When you pull into the gate of Henderson's Farm and Apple Orchard, a long dirt drive leads to his parents'—Dottie and Marvin—quaint white farmhouse on the left. Across from them is a converted silo that used to be Dallas and Beau's home before she married Myer and the three of them moved to his family's ranch. It's now occupied by an old friend, Foster, who works for Myer's family and began renting it after he and his wife split up.

We drive past his parents' home and continue down the dirt road, passing the stables and the greenhouses, and cut down a path that leads out into the orchard.

On the back of the property, we veer off into a heavily wooded area, and Payne's home comes into sight. It's an A-frame-style log cabin with floor-to-ceiling windows that is tucked back in a private nook and looks out over the mountainside. It has a covered front porch that wraps around to the side of the house. A small, detached garage is set to the right with a covered walkway to the back door, which opens up to a mudroom.

I love this place. It's on the same land as his parents, but it feels like it's a separate piece of property.

We park, and Payne grabs a couple of my bags from the bed of the truck.

I follow him in as he hurriedly tosses my luggage to the side.

No sooner do I walk over the threshold than Payne's large hands settle on my hips. He kicks the door shut as he turns me and pins me up against it.

His mouth finds mine immediately, and he hungrily kisses me as his hands slide down and around to cup my behind and bring me in closer. My head falls back against the cool wood, and I reach to thread my fingers through his silky, dark hair and tug. He presses his hard, muscled body to mine, and the heat of him envelops me.

My body trembles with need, and I bring my right leg up and wrap it around his hip, trying desperately to get closer to him. I arch my back, and my T-shirt stretches across my aching breasts. I slide my hands from his hair and down his back, the tips of my fingers digging into his muscles.

He lets out a guttural groan as his mouth runs down the column of my throat, sucking and nipping as he makes his way to my chest.

The need that pulses through me catches me off guard. How can I burn this hot for him after all this time? Rarely has a lover kept my interest longer than a few months, and never has the attraction been this intense. Every time with Payne is like the first time. Just as exciting.

I grip him tighter as his tongue explores the tops of my breasts, which are exposed above the deep V of my neckline. An exquisite tingle shoots straight down my spine as he sucks my nipple between his teeth through the thin fabric of my shirt.

God, that feels so good.

I purr my encouragement as I fight to stay upright.

He brings his head up at the sound, and before I have a chance to complain, he picks me up and carries me down the hallway toward his bedroom.

He sets me on my feet, and before he can even get his shirt untucked from his jeans, I drop to my knees in front of him and reach for the button.

"Charlotte." My name falls from his lips in a raspy plea, and I love the effect I have on him.

I slowly slide his zipper down, and he is hard and ready as I reach in to release him from his black boxer briefs.

I hold the base of him with one hand as I stroke him firmly with the other. Running the nail of my finger down the hard ridge. He twitches in my grip, and his breath catches as he watches me.

"Don't tease me," he says as his hands drop to my hair, massaging my scalp.

"Who, me?" I ask as I dart my tongue out and lick his tip, liking the salty taste of him.

"Mmm, mmm," I murmur, and the heat in his eyes as he watches me almost melts me into the floor at his feet.

He groans, and his hands fist my hair. So, I lick him again, letting my tongue roll around the swollen bulb a few times before opening my mouth and taking him deep inside.

I keep my fingers wrapped tight around him as he glides in as far as he can go, and then I begin sucking as he thrusts steadily in and out of my mouth.

He mutters unintelligible words as his hips flex. I can sense he is holding on to his control as best he can.

I suck him in deeper as I relax. I grip the back of his thigh with my free hand and hold on as I pull back my lips and drag the edge of my teeth lightly down his length. He growls low and deep in his throat, and it sounds like a strangled cry as the speed of his thrusts increases.

I love the way I can drive him completely wild. The ability to bring this strong, rugged cowboy to the brink of insanity is a powerful aphrodisiac.

His fingers tangle almost painfully in my hair as he comes close to losing himself.

I look up and watch his face as he gets completely lost. His breaths come quick, and then he groans my name when I feel his body stiffen as he comes. His eyes are squeezed tightly closed. I swallow him down. Savoring every drop of him and the power I have to make him lose control.

"You're amazing, you know that?" His gravelly voice washes over me like a gentle wind.

I look up to see his gray eyes concentrated on me kneeled before him. His expression is intense, and it makes my heart clench. He is beautiful. Not your normal *sexy cowboy* beautiful, but the type of beautiful that includes his body and soul.

He reaches down and urges me to my feet. I place my hand on his chest and look up at him.

A bittersweet pain boils inside of me. A sweet ache that makes me feel vulnerable and exposed. I've never felt like this with another man. I've never wished I could be more for him. Never wanted more for myself.

His hand comes up and cradles the side of my face, and then he says, "Your turn," before he bends and takes my mouth in a searing kiss.

Thank God.

I don't know how to process these intense emotions.

Payne lifts me into his arms and carries me over to his bed. He carefully lays me down, and then he follows, pinning me to the mattress and settling his powerful body between my open thighs.

He brings his mouth to mine and kisses me deep and slow, and

I claw at the layer of clothing still separating us. Desperate need pulsing inside me.

"I need you naked. Right the hell now," I growl.

But he continues to slowly caress me.

"Payne," I groan his name as I arch up into him.

"So needy," he says against the skin at my neck.

He slides his hands down and lifts, so he can glide my shirt over my head. Then, he takes his time in undoing my jeans and tugging them down my legs.

Once he has me completely naked, he kisses his way down my body at a leisurely pace. Stroking and caressing every exposed inch until I'm a shivering, desperate mess.

When he reaches my thighs, he presses them apart. He finds me wet and ready for him as he rakes his fingertip across me, and then he brings it to his lips and sucks.

Desire ripples down my spine as I watch him.

Finally, he spreads me with his fingers and bends his head, and his tongue explores my hot flesh.

I moan his name as soon as his mouth touches me, and when he nips at my clit with his teeth, my hips jump in his grasp. Every nerve ending in my body ignites, and pleasure twists and knots inside of me as he inserts a finger and curls it in and out. He takes his time, using his mouth, tongue, and hand to drive me into a frenzy.

"Oh, you are a wicked cowboy," I pant as he decreases the pressure just as I am about to fall over the edge.

I sink my fingers into his hair and hold him where I want him. I raise my hips to meet his tongue until I am shaking and writhing beneath him.

He brings his eyes to mine and winks, and then he takes me there. I gasp his name as my orgasm rockets through me.

As I lie there, catching my breath and trying to recover from the moment of ecstasy, he pushes himself off the bed and quickly discards his clothes.

Damn. My eyes feast on him. The broad width of his chest and shoulders and those ridged ab muscles, paired with his lean hips and powerful thighs—it's a sight I could never tire of.

He returns to the bed and covers me. His hot, slick, bare skin on mine.

"Ready for orgasm two and three?" he asks.

"Wow, you're awfully confident. Sure you can deliver?" I tease.

With a sinful grin, he lifts his hips and thrusts inside of me. Filling me completely.

"Oh my. Yes, right there," I gasp out.

He reaches back and clasps one of my legs, bringing it up over his hip so he can move deeper, faster, and my head bears back into the pillow as I fist the sheets on the bed.

He bends his head, so he can kiss my exposed neck, and the sensation of his gentle kiss in contrast to his pounding rhythm is just what I need.

His breath starts coming in short, hard pants as my leg locks tightly around his waist.

"Damn, you feel so good," he grunts as I tighten around him.

He grips my hips as he mounts up and thrusts harder.

I rake my hands down his sides, my fingernails grazing him before digging into the curves of his ass and holding on. He makes those husky, guttural noises that let me know he is close to the edge.

I'm so close myself and aching for release when he slips one hand between us, striking me in just the right place before giving me a little pinch. That does it. My body convulses as I hoarsely scream his name.

Payne loses his hold on control, and his coiled, tight pleasure explodes into me. He brings his mouth to my shoulder and lightly bites down on the flesh at the base of my neck as his climax takes him over.

We lie here for minutes or maybe longer. Me beneath him, taking his weight as I stroke my hands up and down his spine.

Nine

PAYNE

I WAKE UP TO THE BLARING OF MY ALARM CLOCK, TANGLED IN THE sheets, with Charlotte's head on my chest.

"Make it stop!" she groans.

I reach over and cut off the offending racket.

"Good morning, sunshine," I say into the top of her head.

"What time is it?" she asks.

"Six."

"Six? Why the hell are we getting up at six in the morning?" she shrieks.

"I have to get all my work done and then head over to help at the chapel," I yawn out my reply as I click on the lamp beside the bed.

"It's too early," she protests as she pulls a pillow over her face to block the light.

I tug it from her grip and roll us until I'm settled on top of her.

She blinks a few times and then frowns at me.

"Aren't you the one who gets up at five every day for an exercise class?" I ask.

"That's different. I'm home for SoulCycle. It's a New York thing. I'm on a different schedule when I'm here. Besides, it's your fault I'm so exhausted this morning," she accuses.

I kiss the downturned corner of her mouth, and she sighs. Then, I trail my mouth down and kiss just below her ear before I nip her lobe with my teeth.

That earns me a purr of pleasure.

"Tell you what. You go back to sleep, and when I'm done on the farm, I'll pick you up. We'll have breakfast at the bakery before I meet the guys."

My mother and sister own the bakery on Main Street, Bountiful Harvest Bread Company, and they make an array of tasty treats and sandwiches.

"Deal," she says on a breath as I continue to nibble at her neck.

She brings her hands between us and shoves my chest. "Go, before you start something that causes you to be late," she says. Then, she rolls onto her stomach and closes her eyes.

I consider doing just that and blowing off all my responsibilities for the day as I run my hand up the back of her naked thigh to the curve of her perfect ass.

"I mean it, cowboy. You are two seconds and two inches from the point of no return," she says without opening her eyes.

I lean in and whisper in her ear, "See you in a couple of hours, sweetheart."

Then, I smack her bare cheek and head to get dressed.

By the time I get the horses fed and the cows milked, Dad has gathered the chickens' eggs and filled the trough for the pigs.

I took over the day-to-day operation of the farm and orchard when he retired, but he still gets up with the rooster every morning and helps. He might move a little slower than he did a few years ago, but his mind is still sharp as a tack, and nobody knows this land or the crops and animals on it better than he does.

I pull the hose around the side of the house.

"Looks like snow," Dad says as he looks to the sky.

"I noticed the clouds rolling in myself," I tell him as I attach the spray nozzle to the hose.

"You're in a hurry this morning," he observes as I quickly clean out the coop.

"I promised Charlotte I'd take her for breakfast before I head out to help Walker," I tell him.

He nods in understanding. "A pretty girl used to be the steam that made my pistons fire too," he says.

"Used to? I bet Mom can still put a skip in your step, old man."

"She sure can," he says with a gleam in his eye. "Now, go on. I've got the rest of this covered. Tell Charlotte I said good morning."

"Thanks, Dad."

I run in the barn and wash up quickly. Then, I hop in the truck and head back to the cabin. I come in on light feet, thinking I'll find her still curled up in bed. Instead, I find her laptop open on the coffee table in front of the couch, and spreadsheets and other papers are scattered about. A half-empty cup of coffee is cooling in a mug beside her mess.

Her voice drifts down the hall from the bedroom, and I follow the sound to find her sitting on the edge of the bed. She's wrapped in my threadbare buffalo-print bathrobe, and her hair is twisted in a towel. She has her cell phone propped on her shoulder, holding it to her ear, while she rubs lotion into one of her calves.

I stand in the doorway and watch her as she finishes her conversation.

"I don't know. Maybe fifty thousand to a hundred thousand square feet. It needs to be big enough to accommodate manufacturing, inventory, office space, a break room, toilets, and a mailroom. It can be larger if the price is right. That way, the next time we want to expand, we'll have room to grow."

She pauses while the other party speaks when she notices me.

"Perfect. Throw some options together and e-mail them over. Sophie and I will take a look and crunch some numbers. Thanks, Blake."

Blake. The douche in the gray suit.

I met him briefly when I visited Charlotte in the city last December. The guy is a tool.

She ends the call and lets the phone drop to the bed.

"Blake?" I question.

"Yeah, he's looking into some properties for warehouse space for Sophie and me."

"Ah," I say as I prowl toward her.

She leans back on her elbows. "You're early. I didn't expect you to be back so soon."

I place my hands on either side of her hips and box her in. "The thought of you in my bed all alone caused me to rush."

"Is that right?" she asks.

"Yep," I say as I pull the tie that is holding the robe closed around her. It slips open, exposing her gorgeous body to me.

"You promised me food," she complains.

"Don't worry; you'll get fed, but first, I get a taste."

I slide my hand between her legs and gently nudge them apart. I kiss a trail along her inner thigh, and she lets her knees fall to the sides to give me better access.

I run a single finger through her folds, and she gasps as she grows wet for me.

"So beautiful," I say as I swirl my finger around her bud, and her hips jump in response.

Her eyes lock with mine as I bend and run my nose along her opening, inhaling deep. Then, I bring my mouth to her slick flesh.

She laces her fingers into my hair and raises her hips to meet me.

"Yes, right there, cowboy," she groans as she rides my tongue.

She throws her head back, and the towel unravels and falls from her damp hair. Her hold grows tighter, and pricks of pain radiate across my scalp as she comes close to the edge.

"Yes, yes, yes, yes," she chants over and over as her body locks tight, and I know that she's ready.

I suck her clit in deep, and that's all it takes. She explodes.

I lick and caress her until every tremble rolls through her and her breath evens out.

"That was amazing," she whispers into the air. "Now, I want pancakes."

I roar with laughter at her demand. Then, I stand, take her hand, and pull her to her feet. "Come on, greedy girl. Let's get you pancakes."

She smiles, and then she pushes past me and runs into the bathroom to get dressed.

Then, I take her for pancakes.

Ten

CHARLOTTE

"HEY, YOU TWO. WHAT CAN I GET YOU?" DALLAS ASKS when we walk through the bakery doors.

"Pancakes and coffee," I answer as we remove our coats and hang them on the hook beside the entrance.

"Sorry, I don't do pancakes. You'll have to go to Faye's Diner for those," she says as she removes a fresh pan of bread from one of the ovens.

The aroma of buttery, yeasty goodness fills my nose.

"What do you have for breakfast?" I ask before I decide if I want to bundle back up and head out in the cold.

"Muffins, old-fashioned biscuits, blueberry biscuits with a honey drizzle, scones, biscotti, or I can make you a sandwich. The only meat I have left is bacon. I can make you a bacon and egg on toast or a BLT."

"What about avocado toast?"

"Avo what?" she asks.

"Avocado toast," I say slowly.

"Nope, sorry. We don't serve hippie food here."

"Avocado toast is delicious, and if you ever tried it, you'd love it."

"I'll have to take your word for it," she insists.

Payne and I sit on the soft brown leather stools at the counter as she slides two mugs of fresh coffee in front of us.

"Cream and sugar?" she asks me, and I nod.

She disappears through the swinging doors, and I take a moment to look around. The bakery is decorated in red, white, and pink for Valentine's Day. In the display case are several heart-shaped iced cookie options, brownies with festive heart sprinkles, and Valentine's cakes in an array of shades and sizes.

Dallas returns with a small pitcher and a cup of pink, blue, yellow, and white packets. "Here you go."

"Thank you. It looks great in here, Dallas," I praise.

She beams with pride. "Thanks. I've had Sonia's mom working on new decor for every holiday, and I've been coordinating the signature bakery items too. She's making me some shamrock and leprechaun accessories for St. Patrick's Day as we speak, and I'm researching minty green treats. Myer and Beau have loved being my test dummies at home. Speaking of which, I'm trying something new to add to the breakfast menu. I haven't quite perfected it yet, so I haven't added it to the menu, but if you two are up for the challenge, I'll make you one, and you can give me your honest opinion." She raises an eyebrow in question.

Payne looks to me for a response.

"What the hell? I'm feeling adventurous today. Impress us," I say as I slap my hand down on the counter.

"Coming right up," she says before disappearing into the kitchen again.

About ten minutes later, she returns with two paper-wrapped waffles. They are golden brown and smell like maple syrup, but they are dry.

She sets one in front of each of us.

"A waffle? You don't make pancakes, but you make waffles?" I ask.

"It's not your regular, run-of-the-mill waffle. It's a waffle sandwich," she explains.

Payne picks the waffle up and looks at her like she's nuts. "Um, sis, I think you forgot the sandwich part. It's just a waffle. With no syrup, no plate, and no fork."

"Exactly. No mess and no dishes for me to wash. That's the beauty of it," she says. "Take a bite."

He brings his nose to the waffle and sniffs. Then, he timidly takes a bite.

I pick mine up and do the same.

The dough is slightly crispy on the outside and has a light maple flavor. On the inside is folded cheesy eggs and small crumbles of ground sausage.

It's delicious.

"Oh my goodness, Dallas, this is amazing!" I exclaim.

"Really? Do you think it's ready to add to the menu?"

I nod enthusiastically.

I look over, and Payne is washing down the last bite of his with a sip of coffee.

"I'll take another one," he requests.

"You could sell these by the dozen, like you do cupcakes or muffins, Dallas."

"They're harder to make than your average baked item. I'll have to see how well they do and the demand. I'm planning on pricing them fairly cheap to see if I can drive some of the diner's business my way during the week. It won't be a lot of profit at first, but most people who come through the door for breakfast leave with a box of sweets and a cup of coffee."

"Make one for lunch too. Price it a little higher. Fill it with cheese and tomatoes and call it an elevated grilled cheese," I suggest.

"I might just try that," she says. Then, she asks Payne, "You want sausage again, or do you want to try bacon bits?"

"Bacon."

"You got it. What are you two up to today?" she asks.

"I'm dropping Charlotte off at Rustic Peak with Sophie and then helping Walker for a few hours."

"Do you think you could pick Beau up at school for me and take him to Mom's? I have to be here for a wholesale delivery, and Myer has to run to Aurora with his dad later today. Beverly took Faith to Mom on her way to her doctor's appointment and forgot to leave Mom the car seat, so she's stuck."

"Sure. I'll scoop him up and drop him by before I go back to get Charlotte."

"Thank you. You're a lifesaver, and that second waffle sandwich is on the house."

"I'll see you in a few hours," Payne says, and I kiss him through his truck window before I walk up the steps to Sophie's office.

She helps run the business side of her family's cattle ranch, Rustic Peak. When she and Braxton moved into the house he built for them before their wedding, she converted his old apartment above the main barn on the ranch into a workspace for both her and Braxton's sister, Elle.

I knock as I open the door and walk in. Sophie is sitting behind her desk.

"Good, you're here. I was looking over your notes from the meeting with Goldstein. I can see why you are leaning toward his company. These references speak so highly of him. I like the idea of working with someone who built his business from the ground up. There is something comforting about knowing that you're helping a small business and not a huge corporate conglomerate," she says as I come in and drop my briefcase and purse on Elle's desk.

"My thoughts exactly. Goldstein's story reminded me of us and Sophia Doreen Designs and what Doreen said about not despising a small start or something like that."

"Do not despise the day of small beginnings, for the Lord rejoices to see the work begin," she says with a smile.

"That's it!"

"It's a Bible verse. Zechariah, I believe. Gram used to recite it to us all the time. She would say that God paid attention to the way you handled the small stuff in life and that he used it to groom you to be prepared to handle the big stuff. So, if you gripe and complain about or mismanage the little, he will never trust you with more."

"Do you think that's true?" I ask.

She thinks for a minute.

"I do. If He gives us everything we want all at once, we'll break under the weight of the responsibility. If He blesses us in measured steps, we'll learn to carry it as we go. Think about it. If I'd posted my first creation online back when we were still in college and woke up to thousands and thousands of orders the next day, it would have been a disaster. If department stores and retailers came knocking at the door, I would have hidden and not answered it. I had no means to meet that kind of demand. I knew nothing about running a business yet. But that first bracelet sold, and I packed and shipped it. Then, I made two more and sold those at the open market. Then, I went back and made a dozen the next weekend, all while getting my design degree and you were getting your business degree. Now, look at us. We're expanding for the third time."

It's true. We have taken our small pipe dream and turned it into a thriving business. Who knows? One day, we might even have our own retail storefronts. The sky is the limit.

"That's true. I wish I had gotten to meet Gram. She sounds like she was a wise ballbuster," I state.

She laughs. "She was, but you've met Aunt Doe and Aunt Ria, and Gram was a combination of the two, so you have a good idea of what she was like. All that attitude in a tiny five-foot-three-inch white-haired spitfire."

I set up my laptop on Elle's desk. She only spends half a day in the office, and the rest of her time is spent doing occupational therapy with her aunt Madeline, who is married to Sophie's dad, Jefferson Lancaster.

I open my e-mail to find a message from Blake.

"Looks like Blake already has a few properties for us to look at. I'll forward the file to you," I tell Sophie.

"How is Blake these days?"

"His same arrogant self. Of course, his life is about to get a lot more complicated," I muse.

She moves her head to the side to peer at me around her computer screen. "Complicated? Why's that?" she asks.

"Because Mila has her sights set on him."

"Mila? Isn't she a bit young for him?"

I shake my head. "Her last boyfriend was only a year shy of Dad's age. The girl has a thing for mature men."

She snorts. "Blake? Mature?"

"I mean, in the looks department. He's definitely on her level in every other aspect."

"So, are we happy about this development or not? I can't tell."

I shrug. "If anyone can handle Blake, it's Mila. He's not a bad guy. He just needs ... to be tamed."

"Alex will lose his mind if they get together," Sophie points out.

"You got that right. His head will explode."

"Maybe you should warn him," she suggests.

"What fun would that be?"

She smirks.

"Poor, Alex," she says.

"More like poor Blake."

Eleven

PAYNE

I PULL UP IN FRONT OF THE SCHOOL AND WAVE TO BEAU'S TEACHER. She acknowledges me and gets his attention before sending him in my direction.

I put the truck in park and walk around to help him in. I throw his backpack and lunchbox in the back as he hops up and buckles himself in. On the drive to my parents' house, he chatters the entire time, filling me in on every detail of his day.

When we get to the farm, he flies out of the truck and into the front door.

"Beau, no running in the house," Mom yells as he darts past her in the kitchen and down the hallway.

"Sorry, Nana. I have to use Pop-Pop's throne," he calls back before we hear a door slam.

"He's going to rip that door plumb off its hinges one day," she mutters as I bend to kiss her cheek.

"You know he won't go at school. He has to be about to explode by the time he gets home."

She rolls her eyes.

"Just like his mother. I swear, I'd have to go pick her up at lunch and bring her home to potty until she was in junior high school."

I laugh at the memory. Dallas has always been a handful.

"Thank you for picking him up. Do you want to stay for supper?" she asks.

"I can't. I have to pick Charlotte up at Rustic Peak."

She walks over to the sink and turns the water on as she nonchalantly adds, "How is your houseguest?"

"Charlotte's good, Mom."

"And she'll be here until …"

"Until after the wedding. I'm not sure the exact day she leaves," I tell her.

"That's a nice, long visit," she says casually, but I can tell this line of questioning is anything but.

"It is," I agree.

"So, how are things, you know, between the two of you going?" she asks.

"Fine."

"Define *fine*," she says.

I lean my hip against the counter at her side, fold my arms over my chest, and settle in. "We like each other. We enjoy spending time together. What else do you want to know?"

"Do you have any plans for the future?"

I sigh. "No, not really. She lives two thousand miles away. She has a life and business, family and friends there. My life is here. It's hard to make any plans beyond her next visit."

"Oh, Payne, honey, that's just logistics."

"It's more than that, Mom. She's glued to her cell phone and laptop. I didn't even know how to text until she came along. I think she'll get bored of me eventually."

She stops what she's doing and turns to face me. "Payne Henderson, you might be a lot of things, but boring is not one of them," she scolds like only a mother can. "Now, have you asked her to stay?" she continues to pry.

"No, I haven't."

"Do you want her to stay?"

"I hate it when she leaves," I admit.

She smiles. "Now, we're getting somewhere. It's like you're an onion, and I have to peel you back layer by layer. You never make it easy for me. You've been that way since you were little. Dallas is an open book all the time, but you're a locked box." She walks over to the kitchen table and takes a seat, motioning for me to join her. "Come sit."

Great. What have I gotten myself into?

I plop down in the chair next to her and wait.

"Maybe she needs to hear how much she's come to mean to you and that you would like to explore moving your relationship to the next level," she coaxes.

"What level would that be, Mom?"

"Oh, I don't know that. You'll have to decide."

I blow out a breath. "This isn't about you wanting more grandkids, is it? Because Dallas gave you a boy and a girl. I kind of thought that got me off the hook for a while," I tease.

"Goodness, no. Not that a grandmother can't always do with more babies to love, but this is about you, *my* baby boy, and your happiness. Don't think I haven't noticed the smile you wear when that girl is in town. You love her. I can see it written all over you."

Love?

"Oh shoot, you haven't figured it out yet, have you? Oh, I've said too much." She waves her hand about, as if she were swatting the words out of the air between us, as she scoots her chair back and stands.

"I'll ask Dallas to bring Myer when she comes to pick up Beau and Faith. I'll throw together a lasagna and a fresh salad. You fetch Charlotte from Rustic Peak, and we'll have a family dinner," she says.

"Mom …"

"I just want to get to know her better—that's all," she interrupts. "I promise there will be no talk about … feelings and whatnot."

"She's kind of a nut," I warn.

"I know."

"You do?"

"Yes. What do you think Doreen, Ria, Beverly, and I talk about when we're together?"

"I don't know. Baking, quilting?"

"We talk about you children. And then we pray. A lot," she informs.

"We're not that bad, are we?"

"Braxton is doing well. Dallas finally got herself straightened out, and so did Bellamy. But there's still you and Walker. Y'all keep us on our knees. The Lord knows that He's all the hope we have sometimes," she deadpans.

"Walker's about to be a married man," I remind her.

"Yes, but he's still Walker," she points out.

I chuckle as Beau walks in.

Sweating, he says, "Whew, that was a tough one. I'm going to need a cookie and some milk, Nana."

Then, we both burst into laughter.

Mom called Dallas, and she was on board for the family dinner. The traitor. I could feel her smirking over the line when she was on the phone with Mom.

I hope Charlotte doesn't mind being questioned mercilessly. I know Mom promised to behave, but I can see the inquisition coming.

I pull into the gate at Rustic Peak, and as I approach the house, I see Charlotte and Sophie sitting on the front porch, laughing with Doreen and Emmett—her fiancé, Jefferson's best friend, and the caretaker for Rustic Peak.

Charlotte is so beautiful, and I love seeing her with her guard down, enjoying an afternoon here.

But does that mean I'm in love?

She catches sight of my truck, and her eyes brighten. She waves as I pull to a stop.

My chest seizes at the sight.

Shit, I'm in love.

She stands from her perch on the steps and turns to say her good-byes to them while grabbing her bags. She jogs over and drops her things in the bed of the truck before climbing in the passenger seat.

"Hi, handsome. Did you miss me?" she asks as she scoots as close to me as she can on the bench seat.

"Like crazy," I say as I throw my arm around her shoulders and shift the truck in to reverse.

"Good answer." She squeezes my thigh and kisses my neck.

"Are you hungry?" I ask when we are on the road.

"I will be soon. Do you want to pick something up on the way home?" she asks.

"Actually, Mom invited us over for lasagna. If you're up for it. Myer and Dallas and the kids are coming too," I fill her in and wait to see if she freaks out.

"Sounds good to me. I love pasta," she says as she messes with the knob on the radio.

That's my girl. Not an insecure bone in her body.

Twelve

CHARLOTTE

"ANYTHING I CAN DO TO HELP?" I ASK PAYNE'S MOTHER, Dottie, as she skitters around the kitchen.

"Oh, no, sweetheart. The lasagna should be ready any minute. The salad is tossed and in the fridge. Dallas is bringing garlic knots and tiramisu from the bakery. I think that covers everything," she says as she wipes her hands on her apron.

"I can set the table," I offer.

She smiles up at me. "That would be wonderful. Here, I'll get the plates, and you grab the silverware. It's in the drawer beside the dishwasher."

Payne, his dad, and Beau are in the living room, watching television and playing with Faith.

I follow Dottie into the dining room, and she calls out for Payne to open a bottle of wine for us.

Myer and Dallas show up just as he begins to pour.

"Perfect timing," Dottie says as she pulls a pan from the oven.

"That smells so good, Momma," Dallas tells her.

"Lasagna is Mom's specialty. She hand-makes the pasta and jars her own sauce," Payne tells me. "Legend has it that she made it for Dad on their third date, and he asked her to marry him on the spot."

"Is that true?" I ask.

"According to Dad, it is." He shrugs.

Wow, that must be some sauce.

Payne points me in the direction of the bathroom, so I can wash up. I pass a door on the right that has a sign that reads, *Payne's Lair.*

Curiosity has me walking inside and looking around.

It's like a shrine in here. A double bed with a jean comforter is in the middle of the room. A shelf that stands against the back wall is stacked with trophies. Everything from Little League baseball to high school football is represented. Then, there are skiing trophies.

I didn't even know he skied, much less on a competition level. That's interesting. I'm an above-average skier myself. My parents took us on ski trips every year over winter break. My brother is a master on the slopes, both in skis and on a snowboard, and Mila and I can hold our own on the intermediate slopes.

I make a mental note to ask Payne about his athletic history.

I move my attention to the framed photos hanging on the wall to the right of the shelf. Photos of Payne as he was growing up. There is one of him on a motorbike, grinning at the camera, and it looks to be Myer maybe beside him on a matching bike. Then, there are team photos and one of him in midair, catching a football. A prom picture with a brunette and a homecoming photo with a blonde. The teenage version looks as good in a suit as his adult counterpart. I bet the girls were all over him back then.

I pick up a framed photo of him and Dallas from the chest of drawers. They are standing beside an old wood-paneled station wagon, grinning. I never realized how much Beau favored his uncle before. That makes me smile.

"Charlotte."

I jump at the sound of Dottie calling my name, and the wooden frame slips from my fingers and crashes to the floor.

"Oh my goodness, I'm so sorry," I apologize as I bend to pick up the broken frame.

"I didn't mean to startle you," she says as she comes in and takes the photo, which now has a crack in the glass, from my fingers.

"I was snooping. I guess I let my curiosity get the best of me," I tell her.

"I've been meaning to pack this room up and put this stuff in the attic or send it home with Payne for years," she says as she places the photo back on the chest of drawers. "He grew up so fast. They both did. I wasn't quite ready to let either of them go. Marvin keeps telling me to turn this room into a sewing room, but every time I try to clean it out, I stop myself. I sound ridiculous, don't I?"

"I think it's sweet. I'm pretty sure my mother had her tanning bed and elliptical machine set up in my old bedroom before I even had my clothes packed for college."

She chuckles.

"Payne certainly was a busy kid. Talented too," I say as I nod toward the wall of accolades.

"Oh, yes. Everything he tried, he gave a hundred and fifty percent. He threw all his energy into extracurricular activities and none into his schoolwork. Drove me to the brink of insanity. Of course, Dallas was worse," she reminisces.

"I wish I had known them then."

I bet Dallas and I would have been trouble. I don't say that out loud though. I want Payne's parents to like me, not try to run me off.

"I have a feeling you would have fit right in around here," she agrees.

I decide to probe her for more information since I have her attention. "Payne played football, I see. Was he any good?"

"He was proficient, but Myer was our star on the gridiron. Payne just joined the team to play with him. Those two were inseparable back then. But snow skiing was Payne's sport. He was a natural and excelled on the slopes. I haven't the faintest idea where he got it from. I can't stay upright on a pair of skis, but he and Dallas both loved it, and Payne joined a ski team when he was around twelve."

"Does he still ski?" I inquire.

"When he has time. He doesn't get as much opportunity since he took over the farm from his father though."

"I love to ski," I tell her.

She turns her attention from the shelves to me. "You do?"

"Yes, ma'am. I'm not a competitive skier by any stretch, but my parents would take my brother, sister, and me to Aspen every winter when we were kids, and we would spend a couple of weeks on the slopes. It was some of the best times we spent together as a family. I miss it. We haven't gone in ages."

"Nana, we're hungry in here." Beau's annoyed voice drifts down the hall.

Our eyes follow the sound, and Payne's head pops through the door.

"The natives are getting restless in there," he informs us.

"We'd better go feed that poor baby before he starves to death," she says as she motions for me to come.

I take one more look around Payne's childhood room before he clicks the light off, and we follow Dottie.

"This is amazing, Mrs. Henderson," I praise as I scoop another bite into my mouth.

She beams. "I'm glad you like it. And call me Dottie," she insists.

"Dottie," I correct.

"It's Payne's favorite," she informs.

"I swear it could hold its own against Puglia in Little Italy," I continue.

She looks to Payne. "Is that a good thing?"

He shrugs.

"Do you live near Little Italy?" Marvin asks.

"Kind of. It's about a three-mile walk from Chelsea."

"Do you walk to dinner?" he asks.

"Most days, yes. Unless the weather is horrible. Then, I'll hail a cab or call an Uber. I don't trek there often though because carbs."

"Carbs?" he asks, confused.

"You know, pasta, rice, potatoes, bread, anything sweet. Carbs. A moment on the lips but forever on the hips."

"I thought that's what those Spank things are for?" Dallas muses as she stuffs a garlic knot into her mouth.

"Spank things?" Marvin asks.

"Death trap underwear that she and Sophie tried to get me to buy."

His eyes go wide.

"They're called Spanx, and they are awesome. They hold all your carb curves in," I defend.

"You don't need them. Your curves are perfect where they are," Payne murmurs.

I slide my eyes to him and grin.

"You aren't one of those vegan people, are you?" Marvin asks.

"Of course not, Marvin. There's meat in the lasagna, and she's eating it," Dottie answers.

"I figured she was just being polite," he grumbles.

"People who are vegan don't eat meat, period. It's not like eating scrambled eggs when you prefer fried, so you don't hurt their feelings," Dottie explains.

"You're her beau's mother. Women will do just about anything to impress a beau's mother," he points out.

"She's not her Beau's mother, Pop-Pop. She's her Beau's nana," Beau chimes in.

Marvin looks befuddled for a second, and then he throws his head back and erupts with laughter.

"Baby, he means, Uncle Payne is Charlotte's boyfriend," Dallas explains.

He eyes Payne for a moment, and then he looks back at her. "He can be her boyfriend, but I'm her Beau."

Payne chuckles and then puts his fist out to his nephew. "Deal, little man."

They fist-bump, and I get a little misty. It's the first time Payne has been classified as my anything, and to have two of the most adorable men I know fighting over who I belong to, well, that's pretty special.

"Nana, can we have family supper again every week?" Beau asks.

"I'd love that," she replies.

"Good. Miss Charlotte needs to try your other carbs," he says.

"Charlotte lives far away, buddy. She can't be here for dinner every week," Dallas tells him.

His sad eyes come to me. "You need to just stay with us."

"But my bed and all of my stuff are in my apartment in New York," I tell him.

"You can sleep on my top bunk. It's too high up for me. I get scared at night. We can switch when I get bigger."

"Thanks for the offer, handsome, but I'm afraid all my stuff and I would never fit in your room. You don't want all my girlie things scattered all over the place anyway, do you?"

He thinks about it for a moment. "We'll just have to build you your own room, I guess."

Marvin points his fork at Payne. "Looks like you have some competition for your lady's affection there, son. You'd better lock her in," he goads.

Payne looks at me and grins.

After dinner, Dallas and I help Dottie clean the kitchen, even as she keeps trying to shoo us away. Once we have the dishwasher loaded and a pot of coffee brewing, we join the men in the living room. Myer has Faith in his arms, rocking her in the recliner.

"My turn," I say as I reach out for the baby.

He hands the baby over and we sit on the couch, and Beau promptly sits down beside us. Dallas and Dottie join us, delivering cups of coffee and dessert.

I unwrap the soft pink-and-gray blanket from around Faith and inhale the sweet baby smell. She's a chubby little thing. All thick thighs and fat rolls.

I rub the bottom of her feet with the tips of my fingers, and she giggles and kicks.

"Does that tickle?" I ask, and she coos up at me.

"She's ticklish all over," Beau informs me.

I lean down and whisper to him conspiratorially, "That means, when you guys get older and she's getting on your nerves, you can tickle her to punish her."

His eyes go round. "I can?"

"Yep, my brother, Alex, used to tickle me till I couldn't breathe," I tell him.

"Stop teaching my son how to torture his sister," Dallas scolds me from her perch on the living room floor.

"Hey, he's a boy in a world full of girls," I tell her as I elbow Beau in the side. "He needs to know the tricks to survival."

He grins up at me. "Will you and Uncle Payne have me a baby boy cousin?" he asks.

"Um," I stutter in response.

"Please. I need a boy to play with and teach boy stuff to."

The question catches me off guard, and all the playfulness of the moment seems to dissipate in the silence.

"I'm sorry, buddy. I don't think that's a promise I can make," I whisper to him.

"Ah, man," he mutters.

Dallas sees my distress and thankfully interrupts the conversation, "Remember I told you that God doesn't let us decide which baby he puts in our tummy, Beau. Nobody gets to pick out if it's a boy or a girl."

"Well then, we'll just have to pray for a boy, and maybe God will hear us," he tells her.

"Go find your coat and gloves. We need to get home. It's almost bath and bedtime," she commands.

He stands on the couch, and then he wraps his arms around my neck and kisses my head. Then, he hops down and runs off in search of his things.

Myer helps Dallas to her feet, and I stand with Faith in my arms and walk her over to her mother.

"She gets cuter every time I see her," I say as I hand her off, not meeting her eyes as I try to hold back the tears threatening to spill over.

Dallas grasps my arm and comes in close. "Hey, sorry about that. Beau thinks of you as his aunt Charlotte. He didn't mean to upset you or pressure you. He just loves you, and he really, *really* wants another boy in the family."

I wave off her concern. "Oh, I know," I tell her, and I slip my game face back into place.

"Yeah," Myer says as he wraps Dallas's coat around her shoulders, "he wants someone, anyone, to have a boy. He sees nothing but pink princess parties and emotional females in his future, and it terrifies him."

Dallas rolls her eyes at me, causing me to giggle.

She places Faith into her car seat, buckles her in and covers her with a soft blanket. Myer picks it up by the handle and heads for the door. Dottie zips up Beau's coat and kisses his cheek and he follows Myer.

Dallas leans in and gives me a one-armed hug. "You handled your first family dinner great," she whispers.

"You think so?"

"Oh, yes, Momma likes you. She doesn't pull out her lasagna for just anyone and Daddy is obviously charmed, as is my son," she assures me.

I've gotten used to pulling up a chair and feeling right at home at Doreen and Ria's table. I honestly didn't realize this dinner was a big deal.

She releases me and grins.

"Have a good night."

Thirteen

CHARLOTTE SPENDS THE REST OF THE EVENING FURTHER enchanting my father. They chat about everything from their favorite sports teams to what exactly she does for Sophie's company. Which, it turns out, is actually both her and Sophie's company since Sophie made her a full partner when she moved to Poplar Falls. Dad hangs on her every word.

It seems all the Henderson men have fallen hard for the sassy blonde.

Mom loads us down with wrapped leftovers and makes Charlotte promise to stop in and visit with her again before she leaves.

Finally, we are on the road, headed to the cabin.

I look over, and Charlotte has her elbow propped against the windowsill, silently staring out into the night.

"A penny for your thoughts," I say, and her attention comes to me.

"Do you want kids?" she asks.

The strange question was obviously spurred by the conversation back at Mom and Dad's.

"Not this week," I answer.

She doesn't smile.

Okay. Let's try that again.

"Yeah, I eventually want kids," I reply.

"Boys or girls?" she asks.

"Why are we talking about this?" I ask.

"I'm just curious." She shrugs it off.

"All right, I'll play." I give in. "Both."

"You want both?"

"That's right. I want boys to carry on the Henderson name and to pass the farm down to one day, but I'm a sucker for a baby girl," I admit.

"What, you think a girl can't run a farm?" she asks.

I stepped right into that one.

I backtrack. "A girl absolutely can, and if I have a little girl who wants to run the farm, I'll be happy to teach her everything I know," I amend.

"Damn straight," she mumbles.

She's easy to rile.

"So, you're a big-family kind of guy?"

"I love kids, and if I had it my way, I'd fill this farm with ankle-biters," I admit honestly.

She gets quiet again.

"What about you?" I prompt.

"What about me?" She evades the question.

"Do *you* want kids?"

She takes a moment to think about it.

"I don't know if I'd be any good at it. I'm not exactly the maternal type. I'm more *the cool aunt who bails you out of trouble when you make poor decisions* type of woman. Not exactly role model material."

She doesn't know how wonderful she is. She's patient and nurturing with Lily Claire and Faith, and Beau is head over heels for her.

"I've always heard that it's different when it's your child. The motherly instinct just kicks in. I bet you'll be a natural," I assure her.

"Maybe," she halfheartedly agrees.

I pull up to the house, and she exits the truck before I even come to a full stop.

I throw it in park and grab the bags of food. I catch up to her on the steps, and I reach for her arm.

"Whoa there," I say as I gently turn her to face me. "Are you okay? I'm sorry if my parents came on a little strong today. I told Mom not to bombard you with questions. They don't mean any harm. They just want to get to know you better—that's all."

She takes a deep breath and plants her head in my chest. Then, she mumbles, "No, I had a delightful time, and they were great. I think I'm just tired." She lifts her eyes to mine and smirks. "Someone kept me up late last night and then woke me up at the crack of dawn this morning," she accuses.

"If you're looking for an apology, I'm not the least bit sorry," I tell her.

"You're so mean," she grumbles.

"Oh, I'll show you mean," I tell her as I move in closer, and she melts into me.

That's my girl.

I grin down at her and she scowls before pushing against my chest.

"Stop it, cowboy! You're turning me into one of those sappy girls in some cheesy Rom-Com sighing every time the hero grins, and his dimples pop out. It's embarrassing."

I laugh, turn her and nudge her to the door as I smack her backside.

She yelps and takes off into the house, and I make chase.

Wrapped up in the comforter, I glide my hand through her hair.

"What do you have planned for tomorrow?" I ask.

She sleepily mumbles something about work.

"Can it wait?" I ask.

She opens one eye and focuses on me. "What do you have in mind, cowboy?"

I look to the window, where huge snowflakes are falling outside.

"It's going to snow all night. We should have a good three or four inches on the ground by morning. Myer and I were talking about it at dinner. There's a hill on the back of Stoney Ridge Ranch where we all like to sled."

"Sledding? That sounds fun. I haven't been sledding since … well, I don't think I've ever been sledding before," she says.

"Well, that settles it. I have to pop my girl's sledding cherry," I tell her.

She sighs and snuggles in deeper. "Pop away," she whispers.

I like that I get to show her new things. I get a kick out of the excitement in her eyes. She might be a sophisticated city girl, but she is so easy to please.

Another thing I love about her. They are racking up.

Fourteen

CHARLOTTE

PAYNE IS STANDING WITH HIS HAND BEHIND HIS BACK.

"What is it?" I ask as I look around him, trying to make out the logo on the brown paper bag.

"A gift," he says.

I'm so excited that I'm bouncing on my toes. I love surprises. Have since I was a little girl.

"It's not Valentine's Day yet," I point out.

"This is not your Valentine's present. This is something practical."

I don't care if it is. A gift is a gift, and I'm so curious.

Finally, he hands the package over, and I tear it open.

His eyes shine with amusement as he watches me.

Inside is a gorgeous purple down puffer jacket, a cream cable-knit cap with fur-lined earflaps, and a pair of lavender waterproof, wool-lined gloves.

"Payne, these are awesome, but I already have a coat and gloves," I inform him.

"I know, but we're going to be out in the snow all day, and you need more than a dressy jacket and stylish gloves to keep you warm," he says as he takes the hat from the bag and places it on my head, pulling the flaps over my ears. "You can keep them here for when you're in town."

My heart does a flip at that statement.

"Thank you," I whisper.

"There's more," he says as he takes my hand and leads me to the living room, where we both bundle up and put on our snow boots before going out the front door.

Wow.

A blanket of white covers the yard. Icicles hanging from the porch overhang twinkle in the sunlight. The branches of the towering evergreens lining the drive are heavy with snow, draping down to create a glorious arch. It's like a postcard.

Payne comes up from behind me and wraps his arms around my waist. He pulls me into his chest, resting his chin on my shoulder.

"Do you hear that?" I ask.

"Hear what?"

"The silence," I say.

He kisses the back of my neck in response.

"I love it here," I tell him. "It's so peaceful."

We stand together, admiring the view for a few quiet moments, and then he urges me to sit on the top step.

He bends in front of me and lifts one of my booted feet. He takes a flat hardwood contraption with rawhide straps and ties it around the toe and ankle.

"What is that?" I ask.

"A snowshoe," he answers.

"What's it for?"

He grins and looks up at me. His stormy-gray eyes are alight under his long, dark lashes.

"Walking in the snow," he answers.

"I thought that's what the boots were for," I tell him.

"The boots are waterproof and will keep your feet warm, but we are going to be hiking a long way, and the snow might be deep in some spots. Snowshoes will help disperse your weight and let you glide across the surface rather than sink down into it."

"So, they're like tiny, little skis?" I surmise, as he moves to my other foot.

"Yes, something like that," he says as he tightens the last strap and helps me up from the step.

"How do they feel?"

I take a few gliding steps forward.

"They're so cool!" I admit as I shuffle toward the fence line.

I've never been hiking in snow. New York gets its fair share of the white stuff, but it is only pretty for a few hours before it is salted, plowed, and ends up a slushy, gross black mound, piled between the street and the sidewalks.

I look out toward the mountain at the billowing white hills and glistening tree branches, and it's a different type of winter wonderland than New York City.

I hold on to the fence as Payne gets his own shoes strapped on and then joins me.

"You ready?" he asks as he takes my hand.

The twenty-minute hike to Stoney Ridge is breathtaking. I hold on to Payne's elbow, and he guides me through the trees, over a covered one-lane bridge, and up a massive hill.

Walker and Elle, Brandt and Bellamy, Myer and Beau, and Sonia are all there when we arrive.

Beau breaks free from the crowd and beelines for us.

"Miss Charlotte, are you going to sled with me?" he asks excitedly.

I bend down to look him in the eye. He's wearing goggles and a helmet, and he is the cutest thing I've ever seen.

"I sure am," I tell him as I plant a kiss on his forehead just under his helmet.

He blushes instantly.

"Quit trying to steal my girl, little man. I can't compete with your baby-faced charm," Payne says as we join the rest of the group.

I look over the hilltop and down to the mound of soft snow at the bottom.

"Walker and I shoveled in the bank earlier," Myer says.

"Bank?" I ask.

"Yeah, the snow wall down there. It should stop us, so we don't go hurling further into the tree line."

"Oh, that was thoughtful," I tell him.

He smiles. "The orange sled is yours. Come on. We'll get you started," he offers.

I look behind us to see six sleds pulled out of the back of a barn.

Each one is made of three wooden planks about four feet long, affixed to painted steel blades that curl up over the front with a rope connecting the two ends.

Payne is standing beside the one with the orange blades, removing his snowshoes.

I sit on the edge of the sled and untie mine as well.

Once I'm back up, Payne grabs the rope and pulls the sled closer to the edge of the slope. Walker and Elle are already on a purple sled with her seated in the front between his legs. He has his arms around her and is gripping the rope.

"See how Walker has ahold of the rope? He uses it to steer the sled. I'll do the same. All you have to do is move with me. If I bear to the right with my body, you lean into it as well," Payne instructs as Myer walks behind them and uses his foot to kick-start their descent.

We all watch as they sail down the hill at a high speed, and Elle's laughter carries on the wind and echoes in the trees. A few seconds later, they barrel into the snow bank and come to a stop. As soon as they are on their feet and pulling the sled back up the right side of the hill, Brandt and Bellamy get loaded on their blue sled, and Myer gives them the boost they need.

"You ready?" Payne asks once they disappear over the edge.

"Ready!" I tell him, and then I turn to Beau. "You and I will go next time. Deal?"

"Deal!" he agrees.

Payne sets us up, and I sit and scoot toward the front, so his massive size has room behind me. He envelops my body in his and tucks me in close. Then, he takes the rope, and I feel him nod to Myer, who kicks us off. The sled shoots through the powder like a rocket. I can hear and feel the wind as it whips by us, but Payne's warm body at my back keeps the chill from penetrating.

The ride is exhilarating. I squeal into the air and feel his thighs tighten around me in response.

As we are about to plow into the bank, he comes over top of me like a cocoon and takes the brunt of the impact.

Once we are at a full stop, Payne jumps up and takes my hand to help me.

"Did you like it?" he asks.

"It's so much fun. Let's go again!" I say as I help him pull the sled to the side.

I practically take off running up the hill, and when we get to the top, Payne is winded.

"You climb that hill like it was a slight bump in the road," he says.

I look back at him. "SoulCycle doesn't just keep my ass toned; it keeps my lungs strong too."

I wink at him, and he smirks.

"I take back everything I ever said about that damn class."

Beau is waiting for us when we make it back to the top.

"My turn!" he squeals and he runs over to take my hand.

I look back at Payne and he is smiling.

"Looks like I found a new date, cowboy," I shout.

Beau leads me over to a smaller sled. It is neon green and has *The Incredible Hulk* emblazoned on the side. He sits down and scoots back, and waits for me.

"I think I should try the back this time, buddy," I tell him.

"But I'm taking you for a ride like Uncle Payne did," he informs me.

"How will your arms fit around me to steer? I'm a big girl and you're a little fella."

"I'm big and strong and you're not that fat, so I can do it," he insists.

"Not that fat, huh? You're a charmer just like your uncle."

He nods in agreement.

"I am."

"Okay, lil' cowboy, let's ride," I say, as I give in and sit in front of him.

His tiny arms come around my waist and I hand him the ropes. He stretches his neck as far as he can to peer around me, and I clutch the bottom of the sled to keep myself in place so I don't crush him.

"Are you ready?" he calls.

"Ready!"

Payne walks behind us and gives us a kick off and we go sailing over the side of the hill. Beau's peals of laughter fill the air and I do my best to help him steer us without looking like I am. When we plow into the snow bank, I can feel his body launch up and into my back. He wraps his arms around my neck and squeezes and my heart seizes.

"Let's do it again," he requests.

"You got it," I agree.

I sure am a sucker for those Henderson men.

Fifteen

PAYNE

AFTER A DAY OF SLEDDING, WE ARE ALL INVITED TO WALKER'S place for a bonfire and cookout as a thank-you for all the hard work we've been putting in on the chapel.

Myer gives Charlotte and me a ride back to my cabin as he drops Faith off with my parents for the evening. We quickly change, pack a cooler, and jump in my truck.

"Sophie and Braxton are coming. Doreen and Ria are keeping the baby," Charlotte informs me as she looks down at her phone.

We pull up to Walker's house fifteen minutes later. Sonia, Bellamy, and Elle are already seated by the firepit off to the side of the rustic converted barn with a fire blazing. Walker and Brandt are manning the grill. Braxton's truck pulls in behind us. Charlotte immediately latches on to Sophie, and they join the girls at the fire.

I carry my cooler over to the patio and set it beside Walker's Yeti cooler. Mine is filled with iced-down beer and his with mason jars.

By the time the burgers and dogs are coming off the grill, we are joined by Myer, Dallas, and Beau along with Foster and Truett—brothers we all went to high school with, who now work for Myer's family at Stoney Ridge Ranch. They've been pitching in at the chapel all week as well.

Silas and his wife, Chloe, are the last to arrive.

"We appreciate the food and the beer, Walker," Truett says as he loads his burger with mustard and slaw.

"You're very welcome. I wanted to let you guys know how much you pitching in has meant to me."

Braxton is bringing a hot dog up to his mouth and stops at Walker's words.

"What?" Walker asks him.

Braxton sets the dog down and gives Walker a stern look. "What gives? You're being awfully considerate and overly thankful," Braxton accuses.

"Can't a man just want to treat his best buds?" Walker asks.

"Come on out with it, Walk," I say, agreeing with Braxton. I smell a rat.

"It's true. I just want you all to know it means the world to me that you're willing to volunteer your time. And if you happen to feel compelled to help me string the bistro lights Elle wants for the reception out here once you're done eating, I would be much obliged."

"Anything else?" Braxton asks.

"And maybe help me level the spot for the dance floor, but that's it, I swear. After that, it's just beers and an ax throwing tournament," Walker confesses his trickery while crossing his heart.

"I loaded the ladders and toolbox into the back of the truck before we came," Braxton tells him as he finally takes a bite of his food.

"How did you know?" Walker asks.

"I guessed." Braxton grins at him while he chews.

"That's impressive as hell, brother."

"Yeah, I'm a real psychic."

With all of us working together, it takes about two hours to get all the lights strung and another hour to get the thirty-by-thirty-foot area leveled for the dance floor to be set up.

When Braxton hits the breaker and the entire back and side of the house illuminates, the delight on Elle's face makes it worth every minute.

The girls have had just enough alcohol to get up and dance around under the canopy of twinkling lights. We stand at the back of the yard and watch the women singing and laughing. Beau chases them as does Walker's hound dog, Woof. It's a beautiful sight to behold.

"I know I'm an ass, but truly, thank you, guys, for helping me make that woman's dreams come to life," Walker says while his eyes follow Elle as she twirls around.

"And yours," Myer says as he slaps him on the back. "I'm pretty sure Elle wasn't the one dreaming of being bucked around on a bull in her wedding gown, dumbass."

"Mechanical bull?" I ask.

"Yep, he rented one for the reception," Myer answers.

Walker grins and wags his eyebrows. "It's just practice for the honeymoon."

Braxton groans at that statement. "I don't need that shit in my head," he says before stomping off toward the cooler.

Walker looks at me. "What'd I say?"

I just shake my head.

"I thought we were throwing axes," Truett changes the subject.

"We are. Follow me, fellas," Walker says as he leads us to the other end of the yard, where a six-foot backstop with side walls and a target burned into the wood sits.

He takes a key from his pocket and unlocks the wooden box to the left of the stop. He pulls out three sets of axes. All have leather sheaths to protect the blades.

"This is a sweet setup. Did you build it yourself?" Truett asks.

"Nope. My woman had it made for me for Christmas. This set of axes right here are mine only."

He raises one of the Commander Throwing Axes, and the words *Sexy Beast* are carved into the handle.

Truett sighs. "I need a woman."

Foster slaps him on the back of the head. "You need to move out of our mother's house before you get a woman."

"Ow, and you're one to talk. Your wife kicked you out, and you bunked on Mom's couch for months," Truett grumbles.

"True, but at least I've had a house, and I'm not still sleeping in the same bedroom I've had since I was born."

Walker wraps his arm around Truett's neck. "Don't worry, man. I'll help you snag a girl. I was a master at it before Elle got her hooks so deep in me."

"I could use a wingman. Foster's useless."

"Just because I don't want to take random women home from the bar doesn't mean I'm useless," Foster gripes.

"Useless as a wingman, it does." Truett scowls.

"He's just mad because I won't let him bring his hook-ups back to the silo."

"Damn straight. You try explaining to a woman that she has to sneak into your mom's house, be quiet, and hide in the closet if we hear footsteps."

We all burst into laughter.

"Dude, we have to get you into your own place. You're almost thirty. Living at home is not sexy at all," Walker tells him.

"I know. I'm working on it."

"What about you, Fost, you need a wingman, too?" Walker asks, as our eyes follow Foster's to where the girls are dancing.

He looks back at Walker.

"Me?"

"Yes, you. Are you ever gonna make your move?" Walker asks.

"What?" Foster asks in confusion.

"Sonia?" I clarify for him.

His eyes come to me.

"She just split from her husband a couple of months ago. It's a bit too soon, don't you think?" he asks.

"Do you like her?" Walker asks.

"Does he like her? Man, he's been crushing on that girl since the first time he caught sight of her at Stoney Ridge with Bellamy," Truett reveals.

Foster punches his brother in the shoulder.

"Shut up, asshat. She was in high school back then, and I was a married man."

"Whatever, your marriage was already crumbling, and you were giving her googly eyes."

Truett crosses his eyes in a demonstration.

"I've never looked at anyone or anything like that in my life," Foster retorts.

Truett laughs.

"Hand to God, he did."

"Don't let him embarrass you, man. What's not to like. She's a beauty, and she has a heart of gold. She's been an answer to prayers for my mom," Walker says.

It's true. Sonia is a great home healthcare worker and the difference she has made for Walker's mother is nothing short of a miracle.

"You're both single. If you want her, I say go for it. Don't wait forever like this dumbass did," he adds as he slaps Myer on the back.

"Yeah, he pined for Dallas for years and years and then some more years. If he hadn't been such a chickenshit, they could be on baby number three by now," I tease.

Myer turns to me.

"How did I get pulled into this?"

"Just trying to prevent our friend here from wasting as much damn time as you did," I say with a grin.

"You're one to talk. When are you going to lock it in with Charlotte?"

I grimace at that.

We are locked in, aren't we?

"Ha, doesn't feel so good turned on you, does it," Myer declares in triumph.

"Enough of this girly talk. Let's throw some blades," Walker shouts.

Braxton rejoins us, and we spend the rest of the evening tossing axes.

It is fun as hell. Like playing darts, but with the added thrill of the chance of slicing your buddy's arm open.

Sixteen

CHARLOTTE

"I'M NEXT," I YELL FROM MY SEAT BY THE FIRE.

Walker walks up to the board and pulls the ax handles from where they're stuck in the wood.

I stand, make my way over to the box he has painted in the grass, and hold my hand out.

"How much have you had to drink?" Walker asks as he holds an ax aloft, out of my reach.

"Less than you," I answer.

"That doesn't matter. I can handle my liquor better than you," he says.

"No, you can't. Give me the ax," I demand.

He looks over at Payne in question.

"Hey, Neanderthal, I don't need his permission. Now, hand it over," I command.

"Fine." He gives in and places the handle in my palm.

"But wait until we are all clear before you let it fly."

No sooner do the words leave his mouth than I turn, close one eye in concentration, pull back, and fling the weapon with all my might. It hurls through the air and sticks its landing about three centimeters from the bull's-eye.

I turn back to Walker and smirk.

"What the hell? I said, wait until we were clear," Walker cries.

"Oh, you're fine, you big baby."

"You could have disfigured me a week before my wedding."

"Or killed you." I shrug.

"Exactly!"

I point to the target, and his eyes follow.

"Bull's-eye," I taunt.

"No way. That was beginner's luck," he declares.

I reach my hand out, asking for the other ax. He hesitantly hands it over. I turn, aim, and let it go. This time, it lands dead center.

"What the hell?" Walker exclaims as he stomps off toward the board.

"How did you do that?" Payne asks.

"I'm an excellent shot. You should see me at the range with my .22," I say proudly.

Walk returns with the axes in hand. "You own a gun?" he asks.

I glance over my shoulder at him. "I do. What, a girl can't shoot?"

"He didn't say that," Payne defends.

"That's sexy as hell. You terrify me," Walker states.

"Of course she does. She's basically you in a skirt," Dallas calls from her seat.

"Hey now, you take that back," Walker orders.

"You know, she's right. I've never noticed it before, but you are practically the same person," Sophie agrees.

Walker gets a horrified look on his face as he slides his eyes to Payne and clutches his shoulder. "You're dating me, bro. I knew you loved me, but …"

Payne shrugs him off. "Shut up, jackass. I'm not dating you."

"Yes, you are. It's okay, man. I'm flattered, and I love you too, honestly."

PAYNE

The girls and Beau drift inside as the night grows colder, but the men tough it out by the fire, using the moonshine as antifreeze.

"What are you guys doing for Valentine's Day?" I ask the group.

"I'm at a loss as to what to get Sophie," Braxton admits.

"I'm getting married the day before, so I figure that gets me off the hook," Walker says.

"No, it doesn't. You actually have to come up with something extra special for Valentine's Day every year for the rest of your life," Myer informs him.

"Why?" Walker asks in confusion.

"Because your anniversary will always be the day before. You have to make sure Valentine's Day doesn't get lost. It's like when people have Christmas birthdays. You have to get them separate gifts. One for their birthday and one for Christmas. You can't cheat them by wrapping one gift and saying *Merry Christmas and Happy Birthday* on the tag."

"That's stupid. I don't care if Elle gets me one present for both," he grumbles.

"You're not a female," Braxton points out.

"Dammit, that's a horrible rule," Walker complains.

"You were the one hell-bent on a February wedding date," Myer adds.

"I know. I guess I'll have some flowers or candy delivered to our honeymoon suite in Denver," he decides out loud.

My mind drifts to the gift I have hidden away for Charlotte. It's been hard to keep it a secret. Every time we walk past the spare room, I want to march her in and uncover it.

"Why are you grinning?" Myer asks me.

"Because he already bought Charlotte a ridiculously expensive present. I went with him to pick it up," Walker spills.

"Show-off," Braxton grumbles.

"Do you want me to have Charlotte pick Sophie's brain for ideas?" I offer.

Braxton raises an eyebrow at that. "That's not a bad idea. If anyone would know something that would excite her, it's Charlotte."

"I'll see what I can do, man."

He shrugs.

"Thanks, I'll come up with something."

Walker stands and looks down at us all. "Can we talk about something important now? What do you guys have planned for my bachelor party? I know it involves food, and I hope it involves alcohol. I'm going to go ahead and say it: if you guys hired strippers, it's a good idea to cancel them because Elle's already threatened to do damage to my balls if she finds out naked women were giving me lap dances."

Braxton, Myer, and I look at each other while Walker waits.

Myer is the first to speak up, "We don't have anything planned."

Walker gets an offended look on his face. "Are you serious? Y'all can't let my days as a very successful ladies' man be laid to rest without some sort of send-off. What kind of friends are you?"

"Sorry, man. It never occurred to us to plan a party with how busy we've been with the holidays and working to get your venue ready," I explain.

"The girls planned a bachelorette party for Elle. They're taking her to Denver. They're going to spend the day at some swanky spa, and then a limo is going to take them barhopping," he says.

"What would you like to do?" Brandt asks.

Walker shrugs. "I don't know, but I want to do something."

"We'll talk it over. I'm sure the seven of us can come up with a few surprises. Right, fellas?" Brandt says as he looks to us.

"Nine. Don't forget about Jefferson and Emmett. And Pop Lancaster is welcome, too, as long as he can hang with us young bucks," Walker adds.

"All right. We'll plan the same night as the girls. When are they having theirs?" Braxton asks.

"Thursday night," Walker informs.

"Thursday night it is," Braxton concludes.

We all agree.

Seventeen

CHARLOTTE

"I CAN'T BELIEVE THIS TIME NEXT WEEK, YOU'LL BE A MARRIED woman. It seems like it took forever to get here, and now, it's going by so fast," Bellamy tells Elle as we all settle in by the fireplace inside.

"I hope the weather cooperates for you. The last thing you need on your wedding day is to wake up to a blizzard," Sophie adds.

Elle just shrugs. "If we do, I'm not going to let it ruin the day. As long as the reverend makes it and Braxton is there to walk me down the aisle, that's all I need."

Bellamy pouts, and Elle elbows her side.

"Of course, I want you all there. I'm just saying that I'm not going to get upset over something I can't control. Walker is the one who insisted on a February wedding and then wanted to host the reception in our yard. I had to order two-dozen heat lamps for the tents to keep everyone warm, and if the weather is bad, even that won't be enough, especially if we get more snow," Elle tells us.

"Let's just pray that it doesn't happen. The weather is so unpredictable this time of year. For all we know, we'll have a heat wave by next weekend," Sonia muses.

"How many people are you expecting?" I ask.

"The chapel is small, so we're only having immediate family and close friends at the ceremony—basically, just you guys and my aunts, Uncle Jefferson, and Pop—but since the reception is here at our home after, everyone is welcome," Elle explains.

"Do you need any help with the party?" Dallas asks.

"Go ahead. Tell her what Walker has planned," Sonia prompts.

Elle rolls her eyes. "He ordered six hundred buffalo wings and eight kegs, and he rented a mechanical bull. I thought Aunt Doreen and Aunt Ria were going to lose their minds."

Dallas's eyes go wide.

"Oh, and he's making a special batch of his gramps's moonshine for the occasion."

"Well, that sounds fun," I encourage.

"What can I say? He made the dream of being married in my momma's chapel come true. He can have whatever kind of reception he wants. Besides, there will be a dance floor and a band, other food options, and champagne. It will be a blend of traditional and not so traditional."

Elle is the perfect woman for a man like Walker. Strong enough to manage him and laid-back enough to let him be him.

"At least I get to make you an amazing wedding cake," Dallas chimes in.

"That's true. Do you think you can make a groom's cake that looks like an old-fashioned moonshine still? Chocolate cake with a whiskey-flavored soak and peanut butter icing?" Elle asks.

Dallas thinks for a moment. "If you bring me a picture of a still, I'm sure either Mom or I can come up with something close."

"I, for one, can't wait until our girls' trip. Mom made us all the cheesy matching sashes and a tiara with the short veil for you," Sonia tells Elle.

"What's the name of the place we're staying again?" she asks.

"The Brown Palace Hotel and Spa in downtown Denver," I answer.

Sophie and I were in charge of the bachelorette weekend, and The Brown Palace is one of our favorite spots.

"Oh, that sounds fancy," Sonia squeals.

"It's amazing. The spa is to die for, and they do afternoon tea in the atrium every day at four. They have the Devonshire cream for the scones shipped in from England. You dress up and have tea and pastries while a pianist plays. It's heaven," I explain.

"That should make up for the redneck reception," Bellamy says, and we all laugh.

"Who do we pay for our rooms?" Sonia asks.

"You don't," I say.

She looks at me in confusion, and Sophie speaks up, "It's our gift to Elle—the entire trip. Since she isn't having a bridal shower, Braxton wanted to do something special for his baby sister. So, we booked the rooms, the spa treatments, the limo, the restaurant, everything. It's all taken care of."

Tears fill Elle's eyes.

"Don't go making a fuss. He'll hate that," Sophie insists.

"He acts all tough, but that man is a big ole softie," I declare.

"He has his moments," Elle agrees.

"Can I spend the night with Uncle Payne?" Beau asks.

"No, Beau, Uncle Payne has company," Dallas says.

"Please, I'll be good," he pleads.

I look down at his little face and then to Payne.

"It's okay with me if it's okay with you," I tell Payne.

Beau's hopeful eyes gaze up at Payne. He reaches down and rustles his nephew's hair.

"You'll have to help me plow tomorrow," he informs him.

About an hour ago, snow started falling again.

"I will!" he agrees.

"Are you sure?" Dallas asks on a yawn.

"Yeah, sis, you go get some rest," he tells her.

I wrap my arm around Beau. "Come on, kiddo. We're going to have the best time."

He grins up at me.

Myer helps him into his coat while Payne goes to heat the truck up for us.

"Are you sure you're up for this? From what I hear, their slumber parties can get a little rowdy," Dallas asks.

"Yes, Dal, you go and enjoy a night alone with your husband. The boys and I will have fun."

She gives me an appreciative smile and goes to give Beau good-night hugs and kisses. He promises her that he'll be a good boy and mind both me and Payne.

On the way home, Beau fills the cab with nonstop chatter about his day, the party they are having at school this week, and the two little girls who have asked him to be their Valentine. Payne watches him in the rearview mirror and pays close attention to everything he has to say.

I turn in the seat to face him. "Two girls? You are a stud! Who are you going to choose?" I ask.

He shrugs. "I tried to pick Susy because she has pretty hair and she likes frogs, but Lisa got mad and said that I have to choose her because she's five days older than me and she is the boss. Then, she kissed me square on the lips. So, now, she is my girlfriend."

I gasp. "She's your girlfriend because she said so and kissed you?"

"Yep. She even made me hold her hand at lunch."

"You know, you don't have to be her boyfriend just because she told you that you were," Payne informs him.

"I know, but she said if I didn't, she was going to kiss me again," he says as he throws his hands up in exasperation.

"Have you told your momma about this Lisa?" I ask.

His eyes go wide. "No."

"Don't you think you should?"

"Daddy said we should keep it to ourselves because he didn't need to be called to the school because Momma lost her cool on a seven-year-old."

I glance at Payne, and he is trying his best to hold in his laughter.

"That's good advice," I agree.

Beau nods.

"So, what about poor Susy?" I ask.

"I made her a Valentine with a frog on it."

"Won't Lisa get mad?" Payne asks.

"I guess. I'll just have to let her be mad." He shakes his head.

"Women. Nothing but trouble," Payne says.

"Don't I know it?" Beau agrees.

Eighteen

PAYNE

"I HAVE AN IDEA," CHARLOTTE SAYS AS WE WALK THROUGH the door. "We can build a fire and then make a pallet in front of it and all sleep in here tonight."

"On the floor?" I ask.

"Yeah, it will be cozy," she clarifies.

I knew I should have added a fireplace in the master bedroom when I built this place.

"Why don't I bring the mattress off one of the spare beds in here? We can scoot the couch back and make us a bed," I suggest.

"Perfect! I'll go grab our sheets and pillows."

I stack wood in the stone fireplace with a starter log and get the fire going before I haul the mattress off one of the queen-size beds to the living room floor. By the time I have it set up, Charlotte has changed into a cotton pajama set and gotten Beau changed into one of my T-shirts. She makes up the makeshift bed while Beau and I rummage the kitchen for snacks.

When we return, she has hung blankets from the couch to the coffee table over top of the mattress.

"Cool, you made a fort," Beau says as he settles in.

I slide my eyes to Charlotte.

"Feels like camping with the gigantic windows, where we can

see the night sky and watch the snow, but it's better because we have a bathroom."

"I seem to recall you enjoying the last time we went camping," I tease.

Her amused eyes come to mine. "That was a fun night."

Beau's head pops out of the fort. "Y'all went camping without me?" he grumbles.

"It was a long time ago, bud," I assure him.

"Will you take me next time?" he asks.

"We will, I promise."

"Yay, we can go fishing, Miss Charlotte." Beau beams.

"I don't think I'd be too good at it," Charlotte tells him.

"That's okay. I'll teach you how to do it," Beau encourages. "You think you can?"

"Sure. I'm really good," he tells her.

"Do I have to touch worms?" she asks.

He nods.

"Ew, I don't want to," she squeals.

Beau laughs. "Don't be such a girl, Miss Charlotte."

She places her hands on her hips and huffs. "But I am a girl, Beau. I don't like creepy, crawly things. I like pretty things and things that smell good," she argues.

"But you like Uncle Payne. He's not pretty, and he smells bad," he points out.

"Wait a minute," I interject. "I don't smell bad."

He looks over at me and grins. "You smell like horses and sweat. Girls are weird and don't think those things smell good. They like perfumes and flowers."

"That's just nonsense. Horse and sweat smell great," I defend.

Beau giggles as Charlotte wrinkles her nose and makes gagging noises.

"Can we make popcorn?" he asks, changing the subject.

"Sure, buddy."

I pop popcorn while they choose a movie to watch.

Halfway through *Shrek*, I look over, and Beau is cuddled up in Charlotte's lap, fast asleep. She is fully engrossed in the movie, and silent tears are streaming down her face. I watch as she rubs his back with one hand and shoves popcorn in her mouth with the other.

She's a gorgeous mess.

"You want me to get him?" I ask.

She looks down at Beau and then up to me. "Just a couple more minutes, and you can tuck him in," she whispers as she holds him close and runs her fingers through his hair.

I get Beau tucked in on the couch and settle back down in front of the fire. Charlotte snuggles up beside me.

"Are you sleepy?" she asks.

"Not really. You?"

She shakes her head.

"Want to watch another movie? I have *Shrek 2*."

She giggles. "That donkey is hilarious. But let's wait and watch it with Beau in the morning."

"Well, we can't do anything else," I tell her.

She rolls over and props her elbows on my chest. "Tell me a secret," she says.

I raise an eyebrow at her.

"Something that no one else knows."

"A secret."

I think for a moment. Then, I have an idea.

"I want you to try something and give me your honest opinion," I tell her.

"Okay. What ya got, cowboy?" she asks, her curiosity piqued.

I get up and walk over to the fridge, and I pour two glasses from the pitcher I have chilling inside. I join her back in front of the fire, and I hand her one of them.

She takes the glass and looks inside. Then, she inhales deeply and brings her eyes to me. "Beer? No. Something fruity?" she states.

"Hard cider. Try it," I urge.

She takes a sip and then a larger drink.

I wait.

"Do I taste honey?" she asks.

I shake my head.

"Caramel?" She tries again.

"Nope."

"What is it? It's something warm," she notes.

"Molasses," I tell her.

"That's it. Molasses. It's delicious," she says as she takes another sip.

"You like it?"

"I do. Where did you get it?"

"I made it," I confess.

"No shit?"

"Really. It's something I've been wanting to try. I haven't told anyone."

"You should bottle this," she says excitedly.

"I hope to. I've been working on the recipe for a while now. I've been fermenting small batches and trying fresh fruit and spice infusions. I think it could take off. I just want to get it right before I bring the idea to Dad. The orchard does well, but it has a season, like any other crop, and I hate having to lay off all the employees every winter. If we built a cider mill here on the farm, we'd be able to keep everyone employed year-round, and if we were able to sell to grocery stores, restaurants, and bars here in Poplar Falls, it could be profitable. Walker alone would keep us in business," I tell her.

"You've thought a lot about this," she observes.

"I have. My dream is to build the cider mill and then add on a tasting room and small bar. Families could come out to the orchard and spend the day picking apples, having a picnic, doing a cider tasting. We could even host parties and events. Maybe even have live music and cabins or—don't laugh—tree houses that people could rent for the weekend."

"Tree houses," she repeats, and her eyes light up. "Are you serious?"

I shrug. "Yeah, nothing fancy. It would be like camping, only in a wooden tree house instead of a tent."

"I have always wanted a tree house," she confesses.

"Really?"

"Yeah, I mean, I read about them in books, and I saw them on television shows when I was little, but I've never seen one in person. It's not like there are tons of trees in the city. I used to dream of having a tree house that looked like a castle with a drawbridge, so I could raise it and keep my brother and sister out when I wanted privacy. I would ask Santa for one every single year. Of course, he never delivered," she explains.

"So, you like the cabin and tree house aspect?"

"Oh my God, Payne, those are incredible ideas," she encourages. "You could turn Henderson's Farm and Apple Orchard into a mountain retreat of sorts."

"You think?"

"Of course I do. You have the whole thing planned out in your head."

"It's just a dream. I'm not sure I can make it a reality."

"Why not?" she asks.

I blow out a breath. "It'll be a risk. What if I pour all that time and money into it and it doesn't take off?" I voice my fears.

"Then, it doesn't, but you'll never know unless you try. You already run the farm and orchard. You know this land, you know this town, and you know the people. Make a product they like, and they'll buy it. Make it a retreat, and you'll turn that product into an experience. Take it from me; there's nothing better than a Colorado mountain experience. They'll keep coming back for more. I do."

I grab her chin and bring her lips to mine for an appreciative kiss.

"What was that for?" she asks.

"For believing in me."

Nineteen

CHARLOTTE

"**W**AKE UP!" I open an eye to see Beau jumping on the mattress beside me. He is fully dressed and wide awake. He bends down and brings his face an inch from mine.

"Me and Uncle Payne made you pancakes," he whispers loudly and then giggles.

"You did?"

He nods.

I groan and sit up, and he puts his hand in mine.

"I'll help you up," he offers.

"Such a gentleman," I tell him as I let him pull me to my feet and lead me to the kitchen table, which they have set. "Wow, look at this. How long have you two been up?" I ask.

"Forever," he says.

"That long, huh?"

He pulls the chair out for me as Payne emerges with a platter of pancakes.

"Those smell delicious," I say as he stacks three on my plate.

"They're blueberry," Beau squeals.

"Coffee?" Payne asks.

"Yes, please."

He pours me a cup and sets the butter and maple syrup in front of me.

"Aren't you guys eating?" I ask.

"We ate hours ago," Payne answers.

"Hours? What time is it?"

"Nine," Beau chimes in.

Payne fills his own mug and sits at the table with us. "We wanted to feed you before we headed out on the tractor."

"What are you doing?" I ask as I shovel pancakes into my mouth.

"We're going to plow the roads here on the farm and then go clear the ones in front of Walker's mom's place."

"Can I come too?" I ask.

"You want to plow snow?"

"Yeah, it's fun!" Beau encourages.

"Will you teach me how to drive the tractor?" I ask Payne.

"I'll show you," Beau offers."

"You know how to drive it?" I ask him.

He nods.

"Pop-Pop taught me how."

"How lucky am I to have two handsome cowboys to teach me the ropes," I muse.

Beau grins with pride.

"All right," Payne says. "Eat up, and we'll go play on the tractor."

I put my hand in the air, and Beau gets up on his knees in the chair to slap it.

"Is there enough room for all three of us up there?"

"Sure there is," Beau says.

Payne helps me up into the seat in the cab of the large tractor and then hands Beau up to me. He hoists himself up next and moves in behind us.

"Are you guys ready?" he asks.

"Is this thing going to move okay in the snow?"

"It's made for the snow, sweetheart. Plus, Beau and I put chains on the tires this morning for extra traction," Payne assures me. "Now, you see the pedals at your feet? The one on the left is the clutch, and the one on the right is the brake."

"Where's the gas pedal?"

"There's not one. You use the gear shifter here and the throttle here," he says as he places my hands on each.

"Got it," I tell him.

"To start the tractor, push the clutch to the floor and hold the brake pedal. Make sure the transmission is in neutral. And turn the key."

I do as he instructed, and the tractor rumbles to life.

"Keep your throttle on low, release the parking brake, and slowly take your foot off the clutch."

The tractor starts moving forward.

"You keep us steady, and I'll operate the V-blade," he says.

Once we're at a good, slow speed, he reaches over to the lever on our right and brings the front blade down. The blade begins to move the snow up and over to the sides of the drive.

"Yay!" Beau yells above the sound of the engine.

"You're doing great," Payne commends.

We plow the drive from his cabin to the top of the tree line and then move to the orchard road. When we make it to the end and turn left onto the gravel road that leads up to his parents' house, we run into Marvin, who has a snowblower in his hand, clearing the sidewalk.

"All right, to stop, put the clutch back to the floor. Switch the gear to neutral again and slow the throttle."

I do as he said, and he lifts the blade to just above the front end without blocking our view. When the tractor comes up beside his dad, he tells me to set the parking brake, and he turns the key to cut the tractor off.

"Hey, Pop-Pop," Beau calls.

"Hey, buddy. I was just about to come looking for you. Your dad is on his way to pick you and Faith up."

"But me and Uncle Payne are teaching Charlotte how to plow," he tells him.

"I see that." He looks up at me and winks. "We're going to turn you into a full-fledged farm girl if you aren't careful, young lady."

"You think so? That's the goal. I like being in control of power tools and enormous machines," I tell him.

He removes his hat from his head and wipes his brow with the towel around his neck as he chuckles. "That's my kind of girl."

"She did real good," Beau praises. "She's going to be a real cowgirl one day."

"Well, we can always use another cowgirl around here," Marvin agrees.

"We aren't finished yet. I need to remove the chains, so we can take her on the road. I told Walker we'd get Edith's road and driveway cleared for her," Payne says.

I pass Beau down to Marvin.

"I think Nana just pulled a batch of chocolate chip cookies out of the oven," he tells Beau, who takes off running for the house.

"Careful! It's slick," I yell to him, and he slows down.

Marvin chuckles and turns back to us. "Come on, son. I'll help you take the chains off."

We leave Beau with his grandparents and head out onto the

main road. I talk Payne into teaching me how to operate the blade and the snowblower that is attached to the rear of the tractor. We have to drive in reverse to use it, and driving a huge tractor backward is not as easy as one would think. I come close to putting us in a ditch more than once. He's patient with me, and it is the most fun I've had, next to our day of sledding.

Braxton and Sophie pass us on the highway and stop.

"What are you doing?" Sophie asks.

"Plowing some shit," I answer. "Have you tried it?"

"Nope."

"It's so fun. You guys should go get your tractor, and we could plow the entire town," I say.

Braxton starts laughing. "You're the only woman I know who thinks snow plowing is a good time."

"You don't think it is?" I ask.

"We call it work," Payne murmurs in my ear.

"I think it's sexy," I tell him.

"Good to know."

"We're on our way to pick up Lily Claire from the ranch. You guys want to come over for dinner tonight?"

I look to Payne.

"Up to you," he says.

"I think we're just going to stay in tonight, but I'll see you at the office in the morning."

"Sounds good. You two have fun."

She waves as they drive off, and we head back to the cabin.

We take what was supposed to be a quick shower, but turned into one that lasted until all the hot water ran out and I was a shivering mess.

As I towel off I run to the room with my suitcases to scrounge for warm pajamas and remember I didn't pack but the one pair. I think to myself I really need to wash a few things and something dawns on me. I've never seen a laundry room here.

"Where is your washer and dryer?" I call to Payne.

He appears in the doorway.

"At Mom and Dad's," he answers.

"Payne Henderson, are you telling me your mother still does your laundry?"

"If I say yes, will you think less of me?" he asks with a grin.

I ponder that for a moment and then decide to confess.

"Nope, I send mine out. I set a full bag of dirty clothing outside my door every Thursday, and on Monday morning, the laundry fairies return it with fresh, clean, and folded content. It's pretty awesome."

He frowns.

"Mom doesn't pick mine up or deliver back to me. Should I be upset about that?"

"Do you pay her for her service?"

He shakes his head.

"Then, nope, be thankful she loves you enough to make sure you have clean underwear," I say before looking down at my scattered belongings.

"Well, I'm all out of clean pjs. I guess I'll just have to go commando tonight."

He walks fully into the room.

"I'm sure I can think of a few creative ways to keep you warm," he says as he wraps me in his arms and brings his lips to my neck.

Twenty

CHARLOTTE

THE NEXT FEW DAYS ARE A WHIRLWIND. SOPHIE AND I WORK to get all of our reports in order for the accountant to do our end-of-year taxes.

On Thursday, we load up in Brandt's SUV with Elle, Bellamy, Sonia, and Dallas for our girls' overnighter in Denver. Which is a blast. We make sure Elle is thoroughly pampered, and then we get her thoroughly wasted. Turns out, it was a good idea to do Thursday rather than Friday, so she has some time to recuperate before her big day.

I don't remember ever seeing her party that hard. Not that we gave her much choice. Both Dallas and Sophie have been homebound with newborns for months. This weekend was their opportunity to blow off some steam as well. A good time was had by all.

The girls accompany Sophie and me on Friday afternoon to look at a piece of property while we're still in Denver. Blake sent over the information on an old hosiery plant that closed down several years ago and has sat abandoned ever since. It is a massive facility, more like a compound, with several buildings, offices, and open land. It's overkill for our needs, but the price is right and we can see growth potential, so we decide to keep it on the "maybe list" for now.

We drive back to Poplar Falls after our pit stop and head straight into wedding mode.

The guys did some lame night at Fast Breaks for Walker's bachelor party. They spent the evening shooting pool and drinking themselves into a fight with a couple of assholes who were trying to hustle them.

Thankfully, Jonathon, the local sheriff's deputy who responded to the incident, is Team Walker and threw the assholes out. Then, he apparently joined the celebration, and they shut the place down.

I'd say, in comparison, the girls totally slayed the bachelorette party. Thank goodness Elle had Sophie and me to make sure she had a night to remember.

Now, we are sitting in a quaint chapel, which is lit up with candles and filled with flowers. An anxious Walker is standing at the altar with the reverend, waiting for his bride to enter the room.

The guitarist starts to play a beautiful acoustic version of the bridal march, and we all stand as the doors at the back of the chapel open to reveal Elle in a gorgeous antique white gown. Her hair is loose and pinned to one side with a diamond comb holding it in place. Her makeup is natural, and she is absolutely glowing. The happiness and love radiating from her take my breath away. Her hand is clutching Braxton's arm, and he is the picture of pride as he walks his little sister down the aisle.

Walker, the big baby, melts into a puddle of tears the moment he catches sight of her. Which, of course, causes the rest of us to start the waterworks. Aunt Ria pulls tissues from her purse and starts to pass them out to all of us girls.

Elle stops and hands a rose from her bouquet to both her aunt Madeline—who is seated on the front row with Sophie's dad, Jefferson—and to Walker's mother, Edith, who is on the opposite side of the first pew.

Then, she and Braxton stop at a photo of their mother and father on their wedding day, and they each light a candle that sits beside the photograph before Braxton leads her to her husband-to-be and places her hand in his.

There is a silent exchange between Braxton and Walker as he gives Elle to his best friend.

Payne pulls me into his side as I cry tears of joy for the happy couple.

Walker keeps saying, "I do," at the wrong time, and the reverend has to repeatedly tell him, "Not yet, son."

"Someone is impatient," the reverend says as he looks out to the congregation and rolls his eyes.

That turns our tears into laughter.

Once they are pronounced husband and wife, Walker lets out a howl of glee.

He picks Elle up off her feet and kisses her until Jefferson calls, "Save some of that for the honeymoon, son. We're hungry!"

He finally puts her on her feet, only to change his mind at the last second. He picks her up into his arms and carries her back up the aisle and out of the chapel. We all file out behind them. Walker's truck is in the parking lot, and it's covered in paint with an insane amount of noisy cans attached at the back.

"When did you guys have time to do that?" I ask Payne as Walker assists Elle into the truck.

"When you girls were helping Elle into her dress."

We form a caravan and follow them, honking our horns the entire way.

When we make it to their home, Walker jumps out and throws his hands up to stop us all as we start to pile out of our vehicles.

"One minute. Everyone, stay here," he commands.

He opens the door for Elle and picks her up into his arms once again. She wraps her arms around his shoulders and buries her face into his neck as he walks up to the front door and carries her inside.

"Welcome home, Mrs. Reid," he says into her hair.

Then, he spins with her still in his arms and whistles and nods for us all to follow.

The backyard is lit up like a starry night. There is a fire in the pit, and the tent with the food and dance floor has propane heaters scattered about to keep the partygoers nice and toasty.

There is indeed a mechanical bull set up in the far corner, which is being run by a sketchy-looking man named Bubba.

"Is that thing safe?" Dottie asks me as we make our plates.

"Are any of them safe?" I ask.

"Are you going to give it a try, Momma?" Dallas asks her.

"Oh goodness, no," Dottie exclaims. "I'd break a hip."

"I'd ride it if I wasn't in this stupid dress," Dallas says.

"Me too. We should have planned ahead and brought a change of clothes," I whine.

We sit with our plates of chicken wings and potato salad, and I think to myself how I'd love for my mother and Mila to see this. They thought me wearing riding boots to a wedding was insanity. I couldn't imagine the looks on their faces if they got a gander at the menu and when the bull started up.

The band sets up after the cake is cut. Dallas really outdid herself with the gorgeous, rustic four-layer confection standing on a live-edge platter.

My eyes find Payne standing by the stage talking to Foster as I grab a slice of cake for us both. Walking back to our seat, I spot Truett walking up to them with a vaguely familiar face following him.

"Who is that with Truett?" I ask Dallas.

She looks over her shoulder in the direction I indicated.

"Katlynn." She snickers.

I'd forgotten all about her.

"I thought they were cousins," I state.

"They are. She talked him into bringing her as his plus-one. I'm pretty sure it was so she could see Payne again."

"Is that right?" I ask.

She turns to face me.

"Yep," she confirms as she takes a bite of cake.

"Excuse me for a second," I say as I stand and head toward them.

I hear the laughter in Dallas's voice as she calls after me.

"She's a nice girl. Take it easy on her."

I'm not going to be mean. I can't blame the girl for crushing on my man. Who wouldn't?

I saunter up to Payne's side.

"Hey, cowboy," I say as I lean in and lick him from his jawline to his earlobe.

He wraps an arm around my waist.

"I licked it, so everyone knows it's mine," I whisper in his ear.

He pulls me in close and murmurs against my lips.

"I've got something you can lick."

I push away from him.

"Later, I have cake to eat. I got you a slice too."

I grin in Truett and Katlynn's direction before I sashay back to my seat.

That should do the trick.

Dallas gives me an impressed chin lift.

Payne and Myer join us before the champagne is passed off by Ria and Doreen. Braxton gives a somewhat funny and slightly threatening toast that just makes Walker grin. Those two are going to make great brothers.

I feel a tap on my shoulder and look back to see Beau standing there.

"Miss Charlotte, will you dance with me?" he asks.

I give him a brilliant smile. He is the cutest thing in his dress pants, suspenders, and brown bow tie.

"You betcha, buddy. Let's go boogie."

I accept his offered hand and wink at Payne as I follow Beau onto the dance floor.

I laugh and twirl through three songs as Beau shakes his bottom and grins up at me.

Twenty-One

PAYNE

"I THINK MY SON IS FALLING FOR CHARLOTTE," DALLAS SAYS as we watch them dance.

Charlotte's so good with him.

"It seems like it," I acknowledge.

"He's not the only one, is he?" she asks as she turns her curious gaze to me.

"Nope," I agree.

"Does she know?"

"Probably not."

"Hmm." It's all the response she gives, but I know she approves because she has never had a problem in the past with telling me her exact thoughts on any female I acquainted myself with and developed any feelings for.

"What are you planning to do about that exactly?" she finally asks.

I blow out a breath. "I have no idea," I answer honestly.

"Well, Einstein, maybe you should clue her in," she suggests.

The song ends, and Beau comes running off the dance floor, straight for Dallas, effectively ending the conversation.

Charlotte follows behind him.

"I need a drink," she says as she stops in front of me.

I raise the glass in my hand for her to take a sip.

"My hero," she says.

Dallas and Charlotte end up borrowing lounge pants and T-shirts from Walker. They tie them as tight as they can and practically trip their way from the back door to the mechanical bull.

Bubba just shakes his head as the two of them climb up for a ride together.

He hardly gives the thing any power even though it is surrounded by inflated cushions. You'd never know he was holding back the throttle from the way the two of them are hooting and hollering as the machine slowly bucks them in a circle.

It's hysterical.

Dad comes up beside me with a bottle in each hand. He passes one to me, and we watch the girls.

"I don't think I've ever met a woman who enjoys life as much as that one of yours does," Dad muses.

I nod in agreement.

"Beau said she built him a blanket fort the other night."

"She did. We camped in the living room all night."

"And she sure seemed to enjoy the pain-in-the-ass task of snow removal," he points out.

I laugh at that one. "She did."

He puts his free hand on my shoulder. "She's a good one, son. Even your mother gets a kick out of her."

"Yeah, she's smart too. Business-wise. I, uh, even told her about some ideas I have to expand the farm," I tell him.

"Is that right? What did she think?"

"She encouraged me to talk to you and to explore the possibilities."

"I reckon that means we should go somewhere and sit and talk," he agrees.

He and I walk inside the house, where a couple of bottles of cider are stashed in the fridge, which I left for Walker to try. I pop one open and hand it to Dad to try.

"I still can't believe Walker turned this old barn into a house. It's spectacular," he says as he looks around the living space.

"He's clever," I agree.

"All of you fellas are. A lot more so than my generation was."

"You made the old silo into a home for Dallas," I point out.

He nods.

"I did, but it was all her idea. She had the thing planned out and blueprints made to show exactly what she wanted. You guys dream in color," he says, oddly.

I watch as he sips from the bottle.

"How do you like that?" I ask.

"It's different," he says as he holds the bottle up to look for a label.

"Different," I repeat.

We take a seat at the island and I tell him my dream for a cider mill with a tasting room, entertainment venue, and then a retreat down the road.

"A retreat?"

"Yes, sir. I'm thinking small cabins or tree houses."

"Tree houses?" he repeats.

"I don't have every detail down yet, but I envision campfires, barbecues, roasting marshmallows, fly-fishing in the stream, horseback riding—those types of things."

"Hmm," is all he says as he takes another drink of the cider. He lets it roll around on his tongue, and then he looks down at the island in concentration.

"That's tasty. You made this with our apples?" he asks.

"I did. It's the pineapple-infused batch."

"Do you have a plan for this retreat?" he asks.

"Not yet. I wanted to get your thoughts before I took it any further."

He grins to himself.

"What are you thinking, Dad?"

He lifts the bottle and tips it toward me. "This is good, son. I think you might have a solid product. We'll need to look over the numbers, and of course, you'll have to convince your mother that adding alcohol to our product line is a good idea. She'll more than likely spend an extra twenty minutes a night praying."

That makes me snort.

"You put a plan together, and we'll hear you out," he says.

"Thanks, Dad."

"Don't thank me yet," he says as he clasps my shoulder, "and you'll probably need to marry that woman, just sayin'. You're an excellent farmer, son, but she'll be the brains of the operation."

He walks over and places his bottle in the sink. "That's enough business talk for the night. It's a celebration. Let's go spin our girls around the dance floor a few more times before your old man's knees give out. You come over to the house next week, and we'll figure it all out."

"I'll do that," I agree, my voice cracking with emotion.

The door flies open, and Charlotte comes running in, holding her face, with Dallas and Sophie on her heels.

"What happened?" I say as they rush past me to the sink.

"It was an accident. Dallas got mad and started taunting Bubba because he wasn't giving them a real ride, so he turned it up full throttle mid-ride. They weren't expecting it and were slung off the thing. They fell hard, and Charlotte took one of Dallas's boots to the face," Sophie explains as Dallas fishes a towel out of the drawer by the sink and holds it to Charlotte's bleeding nose.

Charlotte whimpers as the white towel turns red.

"Shit," I say as I make my way to her. "Let me see."

I move Dallas out of the way and take hold of the towel. I pull it back to take a look.

"Is it broken?" Charlotte asks through tears.

I touch the tip of her nose, and she winces.

"I don't think so, but you might have a couple of black eyes in the morning, sweetheart."

"Really?"

"Yeah." Then, I instruct, "Sophie, get a clean towel and scoop ice from the freezer into it."

She does as I asked, ties it off, and hands it to me. I gently place it on Charlotte's face.

"Here, come sit down and keep your head back. Hold this cold pack in place and see if we can stop the swelling."

"I ought to go out there and put my boot in Bubba's ass. He totally did that on purpose," Dallas huffs.

"In all fairness, you did call him a pussy," Sophie reminds her.

"You did what?" Dad asks.

She turns to face him. "Sorry, Daddy, but he was being one," she tries to justify.

"He totally was," Charlotte defends her.

He shakes his head and looks at me.

"God, help us."

Twenty-Two

CHARLOTTE

I ROLL OVER AND GROAN. MY HEAD IS KILLING ME. I OPEN ONE EYE and see Payne's bare chest. I can feel him shaking, and my gaze travels up to find him silently laughing.

"What's so funny?" I ask.

He takes a finger and lifts my chin. His eyes roam my face, and then he bends and kisses my nose.

"Ouch."

Oh no.

My hand comes up to cover my face as I remember my injury from last night. I jump up from the bed and run to the bathroom, dragging the sheet with me.

I flip on the light, and then I look in the mirror and gasp.

My nose is slightly swollen, there is a bright red cut across the bridge, and there are dark purple smears under both eyes. I stare at my reflection as Payne comes into view behind me. He wraps his arms around my waist and pulls me back into his chest.

"Just so you know, I'm video-calling my mother later and telling her I was bucked off an actual live bull to get these shiners. I'll probably even take a picture and Instagram it," I tell him.

He smiles at me in the mirror. "You do look like a badass."

"I know, right?"

He turns me around and hoists me up onto the counter. Then, he nudges his body between my legs.

"Happy Valentine's Day, slugger," he says before he brings his mouth to mine and gently places a kiss on my lips. He rests his forehead to mine. "On a scale from one to ten, how bad does it hurt?" he asks.

"Twenty," I whimper.

"Let's get you some food and a couple ibuprofen. Then, maybe I'll give you your Valentine's gift."

"That would make me feel better," I tell him.

"What is it?" Payne asks as he stares at the Nespresso machine with a big red bow on it.

I had it hidden in one of my suitcases.

"It's a coffeemaker," I explain.

"I already have a coffeemaker," he reminds me.

"Not like this one. It makes espresso, and this thing right here," I tell him as I point to the cylinder on the side, "steams and froths milk for lattes."

He purses his lips as he tries to hold in a laugh.

"What? You don't like it?" I ask.

"I drink plain black coffee," he says.

I shrug. "It does that too."

He loses his fight and begins to laugh out loud.

I throw my hands on my hips and watch as he bends over and continues to roar.

"Hey, you wait until I make you one of my famous skinny vanilla mochas. You'll love it."

That causes him to laugh even harder.

I just stand and wait for him to get it all out.

"So, basically, you bought yourself a present for my house," he clarifies.

"Fine, I got it for *us*," I concede. "In my defense, you're not an easy man to buy for. You have all the boots and jeans you need. What was I supposed to do? Get you a stuffed gorilla that sings, '*Hunka-hunka burning love*,' because I was this close to getting it." I hold up my fingers to show him just how close he came to getting the adorable monkey, and then I walk to him, feigning offense.

"I love it," he finally says before he kisses the top of my head.

"Uh-huh," I mutter.

"I do. Anything that makes you more comfortable when you're here makes me happy," he insists. "Speaking of which, it's your turn."

A thrill slides through me.

"Close your eyes," he demands.

I close my eyes and hold my hands open in front of me. I wait as I listen for the rustling of a gift bag.

His hands clutch my shoulders, and he turns me around. "This way," he says into my ear.

And I feel him nudge me forward.

"Are you leading me to the bedroom? Not that I'm complaining, but that, too, qualifies as a gift that is more for you than it is for me."

"Liar. The way you were panting my name last night, I know that's not true," he says.

My eyes pop open, and my neck turns to look at him.

"Besides, that's for later. Now, do as I say," he demands before covering my eyes with his hands and walking me down the hallway.

We make a right turn into what I assume is one of the spare bedrooms, which are opposite of his master.

"You ready?" he asks into the back of my neck.

I nod.

"Happy Valentine's Day," he says as he removes his hands and takes a step back.

I open my eyes and blink when a sleek, state-of-the art matte-black stationary spin bike with a large front screen for online cycle classes comes into focus.

A squeal of glee escapes me as I run over to the contraption.

"What did you do?" I ask as I approach it.

Then, I step into one of the pedals and hoist myself into the seat. I tap the screen, and a menu illuminates with differing levels of celebrity trainer courses.

"It's so you can still enjoy those bicycle classes you like so damn much when you're here," he says.

"Didn't anyone ever tell you that you shouldn't get a woman exercise equipment for Valentine's Day? She'll think that you are calling her fat," I tease, trying my best not to cry.

"Bullshit. I know my favorite girl, and she loves those damn bike classes."

"It's cycle class, and I'm your favorite girl, huh? Who's your second favorite?"

He walks over to me and props his elbows on the handlebar. "I don't want to talk about her at this particular moment."

"Huh. When is the last time you saw this second favorite?" I press as he leans in and kisses the side of my neck.

"Last night."

I playfully push him away. "Ew, please tell me you at least brushed your teeth and washed that thing," I exclaim as I point down at his cock.

He chuckles. "You're hot when you get jealous."

"I'm not jealous. I just prefer not to get an STD for Valentine's too. Who wants to cycle with an itchy crotch?"

"It's Faith. Faith is my second favorite girl," he confirms.

"Oh."

That's sweet.

He looks up at me as I press all the buttons to get acquainted with the machine.

"How did you know what to buy?" I ask.

"Sophie helped me, and Walker rode out to Denver with me to pick it up. Do you like it?"

"Like it?" I gasp. "I love it!"

"There are a pair of cleats in your size in the closet. The saleslady said you needed them in order to ride the thing," he tells me.

I hop off, wrap my arms around his middle, and squeeze. I kiss the underside of his jaw, and he looks down to me.

"I can't believe you did this. Thank you." I sniffle. Touched by how much thought he put into this gift.

"You're very welcome," he says before he bends to take my mouth in a breathtaking kiss.

No one has ever put this much effort into Valentine's Day for me before. Prior to today, the most I ever got was a dozen roses and cliché chocolates in a heart-shaped box. But this? This is something above and beyond, which was purchased especially for me and with my wants in mind.

"It had to be expensive."

"It was worth every penny," he says as he kisses me again. "You can show me how much you appreciate it after I get my chores done."

I run my hands down his chest and over the front of his jeans.

"Oh, I can do that," I agree, and I fully intend to do just that.

Twenty-Three

PAYNE

O NCE WE GOT CHARLOTTE'S BIKE HOOKED UP TO MY WI-FI connection, I left her to a very intense cycle session. She was so into it that she was yelling back at the screen as I walked out the door.

The woman is a nut.

I make my rounds on the farm before hopping onto the tractor to knock down a few trees that were uprooted by melting snow. I pile them close to the barn to chop up later and head back.

In the distance, I see Charlotte walking toward me. The sun is just beginning to set, and the sky behind her is a brilliant pink and orange. I bring the tractor to a stop and watch as she quickly prances to a halt before me.

"What are you doing out here? I'm almost finished," I tell her.

She has a wicked gleam in her eye as she clutches the front of my long duster that she has wrapped around her. "I decided to come show you your other Valentine's gift," she says.

I lean back into the seat. "What's that?"

She opens the jacket to expose the tiny black lace number she has on. It barely covers her beautiful curves. My eyes rake over her body and down to her feet, which are covered by a pair of cowboy boots.

"Do you like?" she asks.

I'm speechless, but I manage a nod.

"More than the coffeemaker?"

I clear my throat and find my voice. "Oh, yeah."

"Good. I've been fantasizing about riding you on this thing since our driving lesson," she says, and I grow hard at the thought.

"You're going to freeze to death out here," I inform her.

She kicks a booted foot up onto the side step of the tractor and hoists herself up and into my lap, facing me.

"Not if you do your job right," she challenges as she wraps her arms around my shoulders and raises an eyebrow.

"Is that a dare?" I ask.

A slight smile forms on her lips before she leans in close and says, "Absolutely."

Then, she crashes her mouth to mine.

I struggle to hold on to her as I tug off my work gloves, anxious to get my hands on that lace.

The tractor jumps forward, causing her mouth to disengage from mine as my weight transfers and my foot slips from the brake.

"Whoa, steady," I say against her neck.

I shift the tractor into park behind her back and turn it off.

"Maybe I didn't think this through," she whispers as I settle back down.

The last rays of sunshine catch in the highlights of her hair and form a halo around her beautiful face.

Damn, she takes my breath away.

I reach up to brush a wayward strand from her face and tuck it behind her ear.

"Don't chicken out on me now," I tease.

She grins, and then she lifts her hips and balances her knees on either side of the seat. I watch in fascination as she shrugs the jacket off her shoulders and slowly lets it slide from her arms.

I place a protective hand into the small of her back to hold her stable.

She is shivering as she makes quick work of my belt and the button on my jeans. Her ice-cold hand snakes in and takes hold of me, and the sensation against the heat of my desire for her sends bolts of electricity up my spine.

"Fuuuck," I groan as she releases me from my underwear.

"Mmm, mmm," she purrs as she begins to stroke me from base to tip.

I swell in her grasp as her fingers work me.

"You like that?" she asks, and my cock jumps in answer.

I bring my free hand up, and with a single finger, I pull the front of her corset down, so her breasts pop free of the confinement. I finger one nipple until it is a hard pink peak. I lean forward and suck it into my mouth.

Charlotte moans and bows her chest forward to give me better access. Her grip on me tightens, and I groan against her breast and lightly bite down on her nipple before moving to the other one.

"Payne, oh … I'm supposed to be the one in control here. You're distracting me," she whines as she arches even closer to my mouth.

I chuckle, and she falls from my lips.

I sit back.

"I'm all yours, baby," I tell her.

She clears her throat and looks between us. My manhood is still standing at full attention in her fist. She lets go, and I fall against her stomach.

Reaching up to her breasts with both hands, she runs her fingertips across her mounds and then seductively slides a trail down the front of the lace bodice. My eyes follow her movement in rapt fascination until she stops at the apex of her thighs. She rises up onto her knees, and I hear three quick snaps as she undoes the bottom of the bodysuit.

She reaches for me again and takes me in her hand, guiding me to her entrance. It's slick and wet and ready.

Slowly, she brings herself down on me until I am fully seated inside of her. Her breath quickens as she rises back up and slowly begins to ride me. I raise my hips to meet her rhythm, trying to hold myself in check so I don't buck her off and onto the ground.

I bring both hands to clasp her waist to balance her, and she gains the confidence to post her hands on my thighs, leaning back until her head is resting against the steering wheel.

At the sight, I finally lose control and start thrusting into her deeper and deeper. She moans my name, and I can feel the vibration move through her entire body.

I've never seen anything hotter in my life than her surrendering complete trust to me as I rotate my hips to hit that spot that I know drives her wild.

When I feel her tighten around me, I know she's close, so I release her with one hand and bring my fingers to where we are joined. I apply pressure to her clit, and she starts chanting my name over and over.

"I'm going to come," she moans just as her body starts to tremble, and I feel her spasm.

I follow her over the edge as she milks my orgasm from me while I roar her name into the night.

I gather her in my arms and hold her close to me.

Fuck. I love this woman.

"Okay, now, I am freezing, cowboy," she stutters.

"Hold on. I'll get us home."

I keep one arm around her with her tucked close to my chest and start the tractor.

I park in front of the cabin and carry her inside and to the bathroom. I set her on the counter beside the sink and start the shower.

We climb in and take our time warming up.

Twenty-Four

CHARLOTTE

"Where's your bag?" Payne asks from the hallway.

He told me to pack an overnight bag with warm clothes and boots, but that's the only instructions he gave.

"It's sitting on the bed," I call to him as I spritz perfume on my wrists.

"Are you ready?" he asks as his big body fills the doorway.

"Where are we going?" I question as I check my makeup in the bathroom mirror.

I did a decent job, but there is really no hiding the busted nose and black eyes.

"I'm taking you to dinner," he answers.

"Where are we going to eat that requires an overnight bag?"

"It's a surprise."

"I hate surprises," I protest.

He walks into the bathroom behind me. "Liar," he whispers into my ear, and a shiver runs through me.

He's right. I love surprises.

"You look great?" he assures me.

"Liar, I look like a battered wife," I tell him.

"Besides that, you look great," he teases.

Fantastic.

"Am I dressed okay?"

I have on a cream cowl-necked cashmere sweater, tan slim-fit corduroy slacks, and cinnamon-hued suede boots.

"Perfect," he approves. "Although I'm probably going to be picturing you in my jacket with that black lacy thing underneath it all damn night."

I turn and bring my hands up to his chest, where I fiddle with the buttons on his red shirt. "If you're a good boy, I might just do a repeat peep show after dinner," I promise.

He bends his face to mine and speaks against my lips, "Stop teasing me and get in the truck, woman."

Then, he kisses me quickly before turning me toward the door and giving me a push.

We drive for a long time, out of the town limits of Poplar Falls and onto Interstate 70. Other than our brief stint in New York in December, I can't remember Payne and I ever going anywhere together alone. I did accompany Sophie and all of the other ranchers and wives to an auction in Fort Collins last year, but that doesn't count.

I watch out the window as the mountains roll past. It's so beautiful here.

"Are you going to tell me where we're going?" I ask again.

He reaches his hand across the seat and takes mine, but he doesn't respond.

"Payne!"

He cuts his eyes to me and smirks. "You're so impatient."

The trip takes about an hour and a half, and then we take an exit leading to Boulder.

I perk up at the sight. I've never been to Boulder.

We pull up to The Boulder Creek Lodge, and Payne parks in front of the main office.

"Hang tight. I'll be right back," he instructs before exiting the truck.

I immediately grab my phone and start Googling the place, but my signal is low, and my snooping is unsuccessful.

About fifteen minutes later, he returns, getting back in the truck, and puts it in reverse.

"We aren't staying here?" I ask in confusion as I watch the cute log cabin–style lodge fade away through the rear windshield.

"We are. I just checked us in. Now, we're heading to dinner. We have a reservation, and someone took a long time getting ready, so we have to hurry."

We drive into downtown Boulder, and it's gorgeous. It's about the size of Denver, but it has a quainter mountain-town feel. Pearl Street is brightly lit with lively couples and groups meandering down the sidewalks. The buildings ooze laid-back charm with vibrantly painted art studios dotted between the restaurants, high-end boutiques, and thriving bars. The city is built around what looks like a miniature version of New York City's Central Park with towering trees and picnic tables scattered about.

Payne parks in a space behind Pearl Street Mall. He comes and opens my door to help me out, and he reaches and tucks my scarf around my neck.

"It might be a chilly walk to the restaurant," he says as he takes my hand and leads me up the side street.

Live music from inside the local venues drifts out into the walkways to offer a soundtrack to our evening. I snuggle into Payne's side and enjoy the aromas of the mix of culinary fare that the city has to offer. It reminds me of the Williamsburg neighborhood in Brooklyn. Sophie and I used to spend a lot of weekend nights there when we were in school. We thought we were too cool. We were definitely too broke for Manhattan nightlife back then, and Brooklyn offered a cozier social atmosphere.

Payne guides us to the door of an upscale fish house and oyster bar, and a pretty hostess escorts us to a table in the back. The restaurant is dimly lit with antique amber lights that hang low from the open ceiling. The walls are exposed brick, and the table has a red rose in a crystal vase and a flickering candle. It's so romantic, I could cry.

The server brings us each a glass of water and takes our wine order.

"I hope you like seafood. It's one of my favorites, and Jax has the best," he says.

I glance at him over the top of my menu. The light casts a smoky glow over his handsome face.

"I love it. Oysters are my Achilles' heel, but the lobster risotto sounds amazing."

"It is, and the ahi tuna and king crab are even better."

I place my menu on the table and eye him. "I never figured you for a lobster kind of guy, Payne Henderson. You are full of all kinds of surprises."

He chuckles. "I'm a complicated man."

We enjoy our meal and a bottle of wine. Everything is superb. Once our plates are cleared, the server offers us a dessert menu, and Payne waves her away.

"Hey," I object. "I wanted to look at that."

The server leaves the bill on the table, and Payne slips his credit card in.

He leans over to whisper, "I have your sweet tooth covered."

We leave the restaurant and walk in the opposite direction of the truck. I lean my head against his shoulder and yawn.

"Are you tired, sweetheart?" he asks.

"It's been a big weekend. Between the wedding and reception, the hangover, our afternoon tractor ride, and filling my stomach with delicious food, I can't promise you I won't pass out on you as soon as my head hits the pillow tonight," I warn him.

"I don't mind. As long as you're sleeping next to me, I'll be a happy man," he says, and I feel the words vibrate in my soul.

He brings us to a stop at a glass-front shop that has icicle lights hanging above the door. The window is decorated with red tinsel hearts and red, pink, and white balloons. The sign above the door reads, *Piece, Love & Chocolate*. The door opens, and a couple walks past us. The scent of chocolate and rich coffee follows them out.

"Oh my goodness," I squeal.

"If you're too tired, we can skip this part," he says.

I release his arm and grab the handle. "Are you kidding? I want all the things," I tell him as a second wind fills me.

He follows me in, and we sit at one of the tables. A fresh pot of French press coffee is brought to us with a charcuterie board of hand-made confections. There are truffles made from beer from the local microbreweries, which are weird to be sure. I've had champagne-filled truffles before, but beer is a new experience for me. Oddly enough, I like it. We also indulge in several cakes by the slice with the salted-caramel truffle torte winning that taste test.

Payne lifts his fork and offers me a bite of the caramel mousse, and I moan my pleasure as it hits my tongue.

"You can't tell Dallas I brought you here. She'll have my hide for cheating on Bountiful Harvest," he says as he takes his napkin and wipes the corner of my mouth.

"Your secret is safe with me," I tell him.

I'm a happy, sated girl when we return to the lodge. We have a creek-side room, and it's rustic but comfortable. Payne turns up the gas fireplace so he can raise the windows. We undress and snuggle into the soft bedding, and it doesn't take long for the sound of the river rushing along outside the room to begin lulling me to sleep.

"Payne," I whisper into his bare chest as his fingers twist in my hair.

"Yeah, sweetheart?"

"In case I forget to tell you tomorrow, this has been the best Valentine's Day I've ever had. Thank you for making it so special."

I feel him lean down and place a kiss on my forehead, and that's the last thing I remember before I'm off dreaming about chocolate soufflé.

Twenty-Five

PAYNE

I WAKE UP TO THE SOUND OF THE JETTED TUB RUNNING IN THE bathroom, and I can hear Charlotte humming. I throw the covers off of me, stand, and stretch before going off in search of her. I find her in the tub, surrounded by bubbles, with her eyes closed and her AirPods in her ears. Her nose has returned to its normal size, but the black smudges are still visible under each of her eyes. The sight of her takes my breath away.

I bend down beside the tub, and her eyes fly open as I run a hand over the slippery curve of her knee.

"Good morning, cowboy," she whispers as she removes the earbuds and sets them to the side.

"Morning," I return as I continue my descent into the water, caressing her thigh.

"You want to join me?" she asks.

I stand and drop my pajama bottoms, my morning excitement at catching her bathing evident.

"I'll take that as a yes," she says as she scoots up to allow me room to sink into the water behind her.

The jets feel good on my aching muscles. I wrap her in my arms and pull her back into my chest. Her hair is pulled up, giving me unobstructed access to her neck, and I kiss a trail from her jaw to her shoulder.

She hums her pleasure as she rolls her head back onto my shoulder.

"I'm supposed to be at Rustic Peak in an hour. I don't think I'm going to make it," she mutters as the bubbling water laps over us.

"I talked to Sophie yesterday. She knows you're not coming over today."

"You thought of everything," she says.

Her lower back glides against my erection, and I groan into her hair. She does it again, this time with a little more friction.

I bring my hands up to cup her breasts, and she arches her back.

"As much as I want to play, we have to get going, sweetheart," I murmur into her neck.

She digs her nails into my thighs and raises her ass, so I slide in the middle of her spread legs.

"Wicked woman, did you hear me?" I ask.

She nods as a needy gasp escapes her lips.

"Where are we going now?" she asks as her hand travels between us to grasp me.

"It's a surprise," I grunt the words as she starts to pump her hand up and down my length.

"Another surprise, cowboy? You're going to spoil me."

I reach in the water to stay her hand.

She turns in my arms and pouts. "Why did you get us a room with a Jacuzzi tub if we weren't going to have time to make proper use of it?"

I grasp her ass cheeks and pull her into me. "You have fifteen minutes. You'd better make them count." I give in.

She plants her knees on the floor of the tub beside my hips and grins at me as she grazes her nails down my chest. "Oh, I can do that."

After Charlotte took that fifteen minutes in the tub and turned it into thirty and then round two on the bed, we finally get packed up and checked out.

Breakfast has to be drive-through doughnuts and coffee that we share in the truck on the way to our destination.

I watch her face as we pull through the entrance of Eldora Mountain Resort.

Her eyes light up as she turns to me. "Are you taking me skiing, cowboy?"

"Yep."

"Oh my goodness, I love skiing. How did you know?"

I shrug. "I overheard you telling Mom. Eldora is no Aspen, but I learned to ski on this mountain. It's a nice backyard resort for this area and the northern front range of the Rockies. It's low-key and family friendly, and it has everything from beginner slopes to steeps and glades. In fact, Salto Glades is some of the steepest tree skiing in Colorado. It's great for intermediate and expert terrains, and best of all, they just installed a new state-of-the-art high-speed six-person chairlift that I have been dying to try out."

She starts kicking her legs that she has propped up on my dash-board in excitement. She looks like a kid who was just told they were going to Disneyland.

"If I forget to tell you later, this is the best day ever," she says before she launches herself across the cab of the truck and into my arms.

"I thought yesterday was the best day?" I ask as she peppers my face with kisses.

"It was the best up until now," she says.

Pride fills my chest that I'm able to give her that. The girl from the city who travels the world. I want to be the man to put that smile on her face over and over again.

We spend the rest of the day in the fresh mountain air. Nothing recharges your batteries quite like an afternoon on the slopes. The moment you step out and gaze down the pristine white top, you release all the stress of your day-to-day life before flying over snow-covered mountains. There's just something about the exhilaration you feel when you're gliding over fresh powder. It's also a great full-body workout. Skiing works every core muscle group in your body, and it beats spending time in a gym any day. I hate that I don't get the chance to get out here as much as I'd like. I used to spend all my free time skiing.

Maybe once I get a full-time staff hired at the farm, I'll be able to take more time for things that I enjoy outside of work.

After we get our lift tickets, we get in line for our equipment. The place is bustling for a weekday. Once Charlotte is properly outfitted, she hurries outside to check out the trail maps.

Turns out, the new six-person chairlift also makes for a great way to meet people. Charlotte talks the ears off of everyone we get seated next to throughout the day and even challenges a few unsuspecting strangers to a race down the mountain. One veteran rider is so smitten with her that he offers to show us some hard-to-find hidden parts of the mountain that aren't on any of the trail maps. I've skied Eldora since my early teens, and there is still nothing better than finding and exploring new terrain or a small patch of fresh snow on runs that everyone else missed.

Standing at the top of a fresh run, Charlotte looks to me through her goggles and smirks. Then, she launches herself down the slope. I watch for a moment as she moves gracefully, like she's one with the mountain. Then, I take off after her, chasing her, enjoying the wind on my face and every twist and turn until we make it to the bottom.

As the sun begins to set and we turn in our gear, Charlotte beams at me. "That was so much fun. We have to do it again one day."

"If I had known you were going to enjoy it so much, I would have booked us another night at the lodge, and we could have snowboarded tomorrow," I tell her.

She frowns. "I have to fly to San Diego with Sophie tomorrow for a business meeting."

"Another time, then," I promise.

"Will you teach me how to snowboard?" she asks, her voice full of hope. "I've never done it before, but I've always wanted to learn. My older brother, Alex, is so good, but he doesn't have the patience to teach me. It would be so badass if I were to get good at it and then invite him on a trip and rip up the mountain right in front of him."

"Of course I will. It'll be nice to be able to beat you down the mountain next time," I tease.

"Oh, please. You held back all day to ski with me. You could have been on those expert terrains," she calls me out.

I grab her waist and pull her into me. "Now, what fun would it have been to be up on those runs all by myself? The best part of the day was following behind you and watching your behind sway all the way down."

She wraps her arms around my neck and bears up on her tip-toes to bring us nose to nose. "One day, I'll get good enough to chase you down the expert hills and watch your ass sway," she informs me.

"I look forward to it," I say as I give her a quick kiss.

On the drive back to Poplar Falls she turns up the radio, cuddles up to my side, and drifts off to sleep. I wrap an arm around her shoulders and hold her close as I listen to her heavy breaths against my neck. She's right, this has been the best Valentine's day I can remember.

Twenty-Six

CHARLOTTE

PAYNE DROPS ME OFF AT SOPHIE'S HOUSE EARLY THE NEXT MORNING. Doreen is keeping the baby while she and I trek out to Denver to catch our plane to California.

The total flight time is just under two hours, so we decided—well, Sophie decided—to make it a day trip.

We get to the airport, valet the truck, and make it through security with only moments to spare. We are the last two to board the plane before they close the doors.

"If we're really tired when we land back in Denver tonight, we'll get a hotel room and drive home in the morning, but at least we have the option to go home if we're up for it," she says as we buckle in to our first-class seats.

"I get it. I'd want to get home to my newborn, too, if I were you," I tell her.

We order mimosas and settle in.

"Do we know what to expect today?" she asks once we are in the air.

"I've been doing a lot of research. We are meeting with a gentleman who works for LG Unlimited, which is one of the five largest luxury jewelry conglomerates in the world. They have more than seventy brands in their portfolio, including a couple of the world's most famous names in fine jewelry. Think Cartier big," I explain.

Sophie's eyes bulge. "Wow, and they want to do a distribution partnership with us?"

"According to the contact who set up this meeting. It surprises me too. I'm not sure what put Sophia Doreen Designs on their radar, but that has to be a good thing, right?"

"Right," she agrees.

Then, she gulps down her drink and flags the server down to order another.

"I don't know why I still get so nervous before business meetings," she says.

I take her hand in mine and hold it tightly. "You got this, Soph, and I'll be right there with you."

She inhales a calming breath and lets it out. "You're right. We've got this."

When we land in San Diego, Hamilton has a car waiting for us.

We climb into the back of a sleek black Lincoln MKT and head to the office building out at the bay.

We look a far cry from the girls who were sitting at a backyard bonfire, drinking moonshine, a few days ago. Today, we are all business in our expensive pantsuits and red-soled power heels. The dynamic duo that took New York by storm four years ago. It feels good.

We pull up to the all-glass atrium, and the driver escorts us into the posh reception area. The woman behind the desk calls up to let the powers that be know we have arrived, and then she guides us to the elevator and shows us to the conference room on the third floor.

She offers us a bottle of Evian water and a latte and leaves us to await the mysterious Hamilton.

Ten minutes later, the door opens, and a gentleman who looks to be in his forties, wearing a coal-gray suit, enters.

Sophie and I stand and shake his hand and introduce ourselves.

"I'm Edward Hamilton, CEO of LG Unlimited. I'm assuming you've heard of us," he says as he takes a seat at the head of the table.

"We have indeed," Sophie answers.

"I appreciate you coming all the way from New York to meet with us."

"Us?" she asks just as the door opens again.

"Yes, ladies, this is my associate Robert," he introduces.

"We meet again, Mr. James. This is quite a coincidence," I say as my seatmate from New York to Denver joins our meeting.

He smiles. "Yes. You'll have to forgive me, Charlotte. I knew who you were, and I was picking your brain on our flight."

"How did you manage to get on the same flight in the seat right beside me?" I ask.

"We have a mutual friend in the city—Blake Thornton. He told me which flight you should be on, and I bribed my way to the seat beside you."

I raise an eyebrow at him. "Impressive. I'll be sure to scold Blake later. What I'd like to know is, why go through all that trouble for a meeting about distribution?"

He looks to Hamilton as he takes a seat across from us. "I'll let Edward take that question."

We turn our attention to the head of the table.

"You see, ladies, we aren't interested in being a distributor for your company. We're interested in purchasing it."

"But it's not for sale," Sophie points out.

"I'm hoping that by the end of this meeting, that will change."

Sophie looks at me, and I give my head a slight shake. This

wasn't what we came to discuss, and I'm more than a little miffed to have the whole thing sprung on us last minute.

"You've met Robert. He's a venture capitalist, and his job is to search out companies that are exhibiting high success potential and invest in those companies for an equity stake. He stumbled on Sophia Doreen Designs and brought it to my attention. I trust his opinion. He has great instincts and well-honed experience in sniffing out companies on the cusp of a growth rate they aren't able to sustain on their own. I took a look at the numbers, and now, we're here and prepared to put a very generous offer on the table."

"Again, our company is not for sale, so I'm confused as to why you brought us here on a ruse," Sophie reiterates.

"Look, ladies, I know you've grown this business from an idea to a vast organization with employees, assets, intellectual property, and a rather impressive reputation in a short period of time. I'm sure the pride you have in Sophia Doreen Designs is priceless, but the reality is, you've already outgrown yourself. You're having a hard time meeting demand from the retailers you are already under contract with, and you are looking to expand into other areas of design. If you get behind on manufacturing now, you will lose the momentum you've built and risk your reputation within the industry. What I'm offering you is a direct purchase that would bring Sophia Doreen Designs under our umbrella. We have the manpower to catch you up to demand and allow for expansion within the next couple months. We want to see the Sophia Doreen brand in its own storefronts. I'm talking the line having its own boutiques in New York, Vegas, Beverly Hills, even internationally. We've had an independent analyst crunch the numbers to determine what your business is valued at. I factored in the value of potential and added it to that number," he says as he slides a folder to Sophie.

She opens it and doesn't give away anything as she looks over the paperwork and closes it.

"This is all very flattering, Mr. Hamilton, and you have done your homework, but we are presently in the middle of a manufacturing expansion, and we're even shopping for space as we speak. I think your assumption that we're not going to be able to meet demand is premature. We've been careful not to overextend ourselves or our resources, and we are actually growing at a very sustainable rate. Yes, I'd love to see our own retail stores in the future, but it's not something I have to have right now."

"Sophie, Charlotte," Robert says, drawing our attention to him, "it boils down to what you want in life. Right now, your company is worth that number to someone like LG Unlimited. The success of a business like yours is directly correlated to the market, which happens to be good at the moment, but you have to strike while the iron is hot. That's what we want for Sophia Doreen Designs. I understand that you're a new mother and you've relocated from New York recently. What we want to do is free you up to do whatever you want to do. LG is willing to keep you on as a design consultant. You are the brand, and your designs are unique to you. We don't want to lose that. Part of the charm of your company is you, the both of you. We'd like to have you both be a part of the marketing campaign, which would include commercials and print ads featuring you two ladies and appearances at boutique openings and even jewelry shows. We would just take over the day-to-day operations."

"And ownership of the operation," I point out.

His eyes come to mine. "That, too, but you'd both walk away as very wealthy women."

"You've certainly given us a lot to think about, gentlemen," Sophie says.

"Take some time, talk it over. Let your lawyers and Stanhope Marshall look over the paperwork and discuss it with your husband,

Sophie. Get back to us next week. I'm sure you'll see that this is a very mutually beneficial proposition for us all," Edward adds.

"We'll do that," she says as she places the folder in her briefcase and stands. "But for now, we have to get back to the airport for our next flight."

"Of course. The car is awaiting you downstairs. We'll walk you out," Edward offers.

The four of us board the elevator and ride it down to the lobby.

"I'll have my secretary give you a call next Thursday for an update. If you need any other information or clarification on our end, please reach out," Edward says as he hands Sophie his business card.

"Thank you. We will," she assures him.

Robert clasps my wrist, and I turn to face him.

"I'm sorry I was deceptive. I wanted to talk to you while your guard was down and get a feel for your personality, to hear about the business from your unfettered point of view. There was no malice intent, and I truly would like to take you for drinks when we're back in the city."

I pull my hand from his grasp and snap my fakest smile in place. "Sorry, but I make it a rule not to mix business with pleasure."

Then, I follow Sophie into the waiting SUV.

Twenty-Seven

CHARLOTTE

"T HAT WAS INTERESTING," I SAY AS WE SETTLE INTO THE ride.

"Yeah, not exactly the meeting we were prepared for," she agrees.

"What are you thinking about it all?" I ask.

"They made some brilliant points, and the offer is for an obscene amount of money."

"So, you want to sell?" I ask in disbelief.

"I didn't say that. We need to discuss it and let our lawyers look everything over, like they said. I'm not going to make any rash decisions."

"Yeah, you should get Braxton's opinion," I agree.

"Not me and Braxton. You and me. We're partners, Charlotte. When I made you a partner in the company, I had a buyout provision written into the partnership, and we don't sell unless we are both one hundred percent on board."

"You did?"

"Yes. This decision is yours and mine alone," she assures me.

She takes my hand and holds it tight, and I lay my head on her shoulder.

"We'll figure this out," I tell her.

"We will," she agrees.

I don't voice my biggest fear. The fact of the matter is, I don't know who I am without Sophia Doreen Designs. I give everything I have to this company, and I don't have a backup plan. Without the office and the work, I'm just a single girl in her thirties in an apartment in New York City with no direction in life. I don't even have a pet. What would I do?

After a few moments of silence, Sophie interrupts my thoughts. "What about that ass, Robert James?"

"Oh my God, right?! What a sneaky bastard! And you wait until I get my hands on Blake," I declare.

We decide to make the drive back to Poplar Falls. While Sophie and I wait for the valet to bring her truck around, I make a call.

"Blake Thornton," he answers the phone like he has no idea who's calling.

"You pronounced *snake in the grass* wrong," I hiss over the line.

"Charlotte, it's always a treat to hear your voice."

"Bite me, traitor."

He chuckles. "Pray tell, may I ask, what have I done to piss you off this time?"

"Like you don't know."

"I honestly don't have the faintest idea, Charlotte, and I'm too busy for riddles at the moment."

"Sophie and I had an interesting meeting this afternoon and imagine my surprise when it was interrupted by a mutual friend of ours. Does the name Robert James ring a bell?"

"Of course it does. I'm Robert's personal trader."

"Want to tell me why you sent him sniffing around me and my company?"

"You're being a little dramatic, Charlotte. I didn't send him anywhere. He was in my office when you called for an update on the city licenses. He had heard of Sophia Doreen Designs, and I bragged about you for a bit—that's all."

"Then, how did he end up on the same flight as I did?"

"I have no idea."

"Well, he said he got the information from you."

"I don't know what to tell you. I didn't give him any personal information about you. We talked business, and then I walked him out. I was meeting Mila for lunch, and she was waiting for me in the lobby."

"Mila?"

"Yes, she was shooting something for a magazine down by the wharf and asked if I wanted to have lunch with her and some other girls, but we ended up dining with a sleazy photographer who couldn't keep his paws off her. The man had to be old enough to be her father. It was rather disturbing. I made it a point to meet her that evening to make sure she made it home safely."

"Mila's a big girl who can handle herself."

"She's young, beautiful, ambitious, and naive. That's a dangerous combination for someone in her industry. There are monsters around every corner, waiting to take advantage of a girl like her."

Looks like my baby sister has her mouse on the string.

"Back to Robert," I redirect our conversation.

"Yes, Robert, right. We went downstairs, and I introduced him to Mila. He waited with her while I pulled the car around, and that was that."

"You had no idea that he and his associates wanted to acquire Sophia Doreen Designs?"

"I've known Robert for years. He's a shrewd entrepreneur, and he was extremely interested in you. Of course, I had some inkling, but, Charlotte, he's smart, and he and his friends have deep pockets. I thought you and Sophie would consider it flattering."

Ugh. He sounds sincere.

"It is flattering, but we weren't interested in selling."

"Then, it's settled. I found a few more properties for you to take a look at in addition to the ones I sent earlier this week. I'll forward those to you this afternoon. When will you be back in the city?"

"I fly in this weekend."

"I'll have my secretary check my calendar, and we'll get together next week and go over the pros and cons of each location."

"Sounds good. Thanks, Blake."

"You're welcome. See you soon."

I disconnect and stare at the phone. I really wanted to be angry with him. I need someone to be angry with, but he's right; I should consider it a compliment that people like Robert and Edward are noticing our company, not let it piss me off.

What is going on with me?

It's late when we pull in at Sophie's house, but Payne's truck is in the drive. I'm happy to see it. It's been an emotionally draining day, and all I want to do is get back to the cabin, kick off these shoes, and take a hot shower.

When we walk in the back door, we find the boys in front of the television with Lily Claire in Payne's lap.

"Hey, how did it go?" Braxton asks as he scoots over for Sophie to drop on the couch beside him.

"Not as we planned," she answers.

"Is that good or bad?" he asks.

"Neither. I'll explain it later. I'm exhausted."

He brings his hand up and massages the back of her neck, and she sighs and leans into his touch.

"I'm beat too. Take me home, cowboy?" I ask.

"Yes, ma'am," he says as he passes the baby to Sophie.

"I'll see you tomorrow, Soph," I say as I let Payne guide us to the door.

"Okay, good night," she calls.

Braxton follows us and stands at the door as we make our way to the truck.

Payne waves to him as we back out, and Braxton closes the door and turns out the porch lights.

"I take it, it was a tough day?" Payne observes.

"It was a long day. I don't think I'm meant for all this driving and flying in a twelve-hour time span," I tell him.

He lays his arm on the seat behind my head and scoots me closer to him. "You relax, and when we get home, I'll build us a fire and open a bottle of wine while you get comfortable," he proposes.

I lay my head on his shoulder and let the weight of the day fall away as he runs his fingers through my hair. I'm so grateful that I'm here and I have him to curl up with tonight.

"That sounds wonderful," I tell him.

"Are you hungry?" he asks.

"I could eat. Sophie and I choked down some tasteless airport food before we boarded our flight back to Denver, but that's all I've had today."

"How about we stop in town and grab a pizza?" he suggests.

My stomach growls in favor of this idea.

"I'll take that as a yes."

He chuckles as he pulls a U-turn.

Crazy HEARTS

When we finally make it home, I quickly shower and throw on one of Payne's T-shirts that I fished out of his chest of drawers. When I meet him in the living room, he has the fire going, the pizza box opened on the coffee table with a stack of paper towels, and a bottle of red wine breathing.

I take a seat beside him on the couch and grab a slice.

"I know it's not New York pizza, but it's a pretty damn good wood-fired pie," he says as I take a bite.

He watches as I chew.

"Well?"

"It's really tasty," I praise.

He smiles. "Glad you like it."

We finish eating, and I pick out a movie to watch. I curl into Payne's side as he takes the blanket that's lying on the back of the couch and covers us with it.

"I'm going over to Dad's tomorrow to talk to him about the ci-der mill," he says as the opening credits begin to scroll across the screen.

"You are? How did that come about?" I ask.

"I told him my ideas the other night at Walker and Elle's recep-tion, and I let him try one of the hard ciders. He appeared to be im-pressed and willing to consider the addition. He said he'd talk it over with Mom, and he wanted us to meet and discuss it further."

"That's exciting."

"Yep. Do you think you could go with me?" he asks.

"Me?"

"Yes, I have the plans in my head, but I'm not that articulate when it comes to the actual business part. You're the smartest person

I know, and you run a successful business. We could use your insight and advice."

A warm feeling settles over me as his praise lingers in the air. He has no idea how much I needed to hear it tonight, but somehow, he always says the right thing.

"Of course I'll go with you. The cider mill is a good idea. Expanding the farm to include entertainment is an even better idea. You have no reason to be nervous," I reassure him.

He kisses me long and slow in reply. Then, he coaxes my head back down to his chest and wraps me in his arms as we watch our movie.

I don't make it five minutes in before I lose my fight and fall fast asleep.

I awaken sometime in the night and blink at the last embers glowing in the fireplace. The television is off, and Payne's head is resting on the back of the couch. His eyes are closed, and he is lightly snoring. His arm is still holding me to him. His body is warm, and I'm so comfortable, but I don't want him to sleep in that position all night. So, I slip my hand under his shirt and run my fingers through the patch of dark curls on his chest, and he stirs. I tug gently, and one of his eyes pops open and looks at me.

"Let's go to bed, cowboy," I say once I know he is awake.

"I'm exhausted, woman. You'll just have to crawl on and have at it," he says before closing his eye again.

I giggle.

"No, I mean, go to bed. To sleep," I whisper.

His arms tighten around me.

"Payne," I call as I wiggle free and stand.

He opens his eyes once again, and I reach for his hands and pull with all my strength. His massive body barely budges.

He counters, and I fall on top of him.

"All right, if you insist," he says before taking my mouth in a deep kiss.

I melt into him and wrap my arms and legs around him.

He stands without disengaging and carries us to the bedroom.

Then, I crawl on top of him and have at it.

Twenty-Eight

PAYNE

CHARLOTTE AND I ARE GOING TO HAVE BREAKFAST WITH MOM and Dad this morning.

We awake early and sit at my kitchen table, and we get a makeshift presentation together, complete with a rough sketch of the layout of the cider mill, the tasting room and bar, shop, and picnic area. Charlotte pulls together some budgetary numbers and preliminary interest rates for reference, and I pack a few bottles of hard cider in different flavors.

When we walk into the house, Mom has the eat-in table set with platters of biscuits, bacon, scrambled eggs, grits, and sausage gravy waiting.

Dad joins us, and as we sit and eat, we start discussing the plans I have for the farm.

Both Mom and Dad listen intently as I give them a step-by-step timeline for the expansion. Charlotte goes over the financials with them next, and then I bring it home with the profit forecasts for the next few years.

"Charlotte suggests building the cider mill first because we could work on it in the spring. That way, it'd be ready by fall harvest. It takes about two weeks for cider to ferment, so we could do a soft open to see how it goes. If it looks like it's viable, we could take out a business loan against the farm and build the tasting room and bar. She even suggested partnering with Dallas and the bakery to add sandwiches and baked goods to the menu. It could turn into something that would keep our regular seasonal employees on year-round and be profitable for both the farm and Bountiful Harvest Bread Company."

Mom and Dad are looking at each other across the table, having one of the silent conversations that they have had my entire life.

Charlotte speaks up next.

"I put a few numbers together for you to look over."

She hands Dad the paperwork.

"We sketched the layout too. The mill would be here," she says as she points to the drawing.

"The tasting room would be on the front and it would open up to this courtyard overlooking the orchard," I add.

"Is there room for all that?" Mom asks.

"Absolutely," I assure her.

She stares at the paper like she's trying to envision it.

"Close your eyes and picture a warm summer night," Charlotte prompts and Mom looks to me before she does as she's asked.

"Now, imagine a courtyard strung with twinkling lights, in the center stands a stone fire pit, there is a small outdoor stage for live music on one side, picnic tables for families to eat around on the other, and maybe a couple food trucks parked on the outer edge. Can't you hear the children's laughter as they enjoy an evening with their mom and dad under the stars?"

"I can," Mom whispers.

Dad is watching Charlotte as she describes the scene.

Mom opens her eyes and smiles at me.

"Dad?" I call.

He cuts his eyes to me.

"What do you think?" I ask.

"Do you know that when I took over the farm from your grandfather some forty—wow, forty—years ago, it was just a tomato farm? It was fine when you kids were little. It kept food on the table and a roof over our heads, but then you kids turned into teenagers who needed braces and football gear and money for cheerleading camp. That was when I decided to clear the back hundred acres and plant apple trees. I remember my dad telling me I was crazy and that an orchard would never survive in the Rocky Mountains," he begins.

I vaguely remember Grandad not being a fan of the orchard idea.

"We had a very tense relationship after that. The orchard struggled. That first year, I lost half the trees to an early frost because I had no idea what I was doing, but I kept going, and I learned my lessons the hard way. I got better at it, and eventually, the orchard started thriving. Before he passed, he told me he was sorry and that it wasn't that he didn't believe in me; it was that he was scared I'd fail and that he'd be too old and feeble to be able to do anything to help me."

"Do you think I'll fail?" I ask.

"No. I think you're smart, and you're a hard worker with a dream. Every father hopes his son will take what they've built and make it better, stronger, to hand down to his own son one day. That's all we can ask—that each generation takes what we give them, what we teach them, and does something better than we did."

I look from him to Mom.

She smiles and gives Dad a nod.

"I guess we'd better get to work on clearing the spot if you want to start construction on that mill by spring," he says.

Charlotte's hand comes to my arm, and she squeezes.

"Thank you, Dad, Mom. I won't let you down," I promise.

"We know you won't, son," Mom says. "I can't wait till the time comes to talk to your sister about incorporating the bakery into the mill. I love the idea of you two working together to build a legacy for our grandchildren. Maybe, Bountiful Harvest can even invest in one of those food trucks you mentioned, Charlotte."

"That will be next year sometime, but I agree. The dream is to develop this farm into a business that will sustain our family for generations to come," I tell her.

When we finish up with Mom and Dad, I take Charlotte to drop her off at Rustic Peak, so she can get some work in with Sophie.

"That went great!" she states as we climb into the truck.

"It did. Thanks to you," I tell her.

She waves off my gratitude. "All I did was look up a few details. It was all you. Your plans and your dream. You impressed them. I could see the pride rolling off your dad."

I reach over, take her hand in mine, bring it to my lips, and kiss her wrist.

She smiles a weak smile and turns to stare out the window.

Something is off with her. She hasn't been herself since she returned from California. I don't want to push, but I wish she'd share with me. I want to be there for her the same way she is there for me.

"Are you okay?" I ask.

"Just feeling a bit lost at the moment," she mutters.

"Why's that?"

She shrugs.

"Come on, Charlotte. Talk to me," I press.

"A large jewelry company made an offer to buy us out. It's not a done deal. I'm just torn on what I want to do, and I don't want to make the wrong decision based on my wants and not taking what's best for Sophie and her family into consideration. I guess I'm just processing."

"I'm sorry, sweetheart," I say.

"Yeah, poor me. Do I keep my successful business, or do I sell for a sizable chunk of cash and not have to work again? Everyone should have to face such horrible dilemmas." She makes light of the situation.

"You're allowed to feel the way you do, Charlotte. It's not just about Sophie. You give as much as, if not more than, she does to the company. You don't have a thing to feel guilty about because you're questioning what to do. I'm sure Sophie understands," I assure her.

She brings her eyes to mine. "You don't think I'm being selfish?"

"No."

"I hate change. It's one of my character flaws. I thought I was getting better with it, what with the whole *best friend of twenty years and business partner up and moving away in the spur of the moment and leaving me all by myself* thing, but I guess I was kidding myself."

"You hate change? You, the woman who encouraged me to change up my entire business? The one who loves surprises?"

"I'm an enigma. What can I say?" she declares.

"That you are, Charlotte Claiborne. That you are."

Twenty-Nine

CHARLOTTE

I WALK INTO THE KITCHEN AT RUSTIC PEAK TO FIND SOPHIE SITTING at the table with a cup of coffee, looking over the contents of the folder from yesterday.

I make my way to the cupboard and pull out a mug. I pour myself coffee and sit down opposite her.

"Any luck?" I ask as I eye the folder.

She closes it and looks me in the eye. "I'm thinking we pass," she says, and the knot that was in my chest starts to dissipate.

"Did you talk to Braxton about it?" I ask, wanting to make sure she's thought it through.

"I did. He's on board either way, and I could tell you didn't want to sell. So, we'll continue our partnership. It's worked well for us so far," she explains.

"Are you absolutely sure you want to decline?"

She nods. "I'm absolutely sure."

I can't hide the relief that I feel.

"So, we'll keep looking for properties. And Blake will be offering us his services for free," I announce.

"Oh, he'll love that," she teases.

"It's what he deserves. I'm meeting him in the city, and I'll tell him to step it up. I expect him to have several walk-throughs planned for me for next week."

She frowns.

"What?" I ask, alarmed.

"I don't like to think about you leaving. It seems like I just picked you up from the airport."

"I know. I leave the day after tomorrow. Time flies when you're having fun."

I don't even want to think about packing again.

Doreen invites Payne and me to stay for dinner. Since she is making her famous pot roast, I agree. I need to taste this mystical *roasted beef and potato* combination to see what all the fuss is about.

Doreen and Ria let Sophie and me help in the kitchen once we are done working. I'm once again on onion duty, but instead of dicing, I'm instructed to peel and quarter them while Sophie peels and slices carrots from Ria's garden.

I didn't think carrots grew in the winter, but apparently, Ria has a magical green thumb and can get anything to grow just about year-round.

"I wish I were more domesticated," I tell Doreen as I hand her the onions.

"Do you really?" she asks with a raised eyebrow.

"More like I wish that I wanted to be more domesticated," I admit.

She chuckles.

"That's what I thought."

"I can't even make breakfast. I'm so used to grabbing a bagel and pressed juice at the café on the corner on the way to the office and the farm doesn't have a corner café. Payne and I have eaten

Pop-Tarts the last few mornings, and he doesn't even own a toaster, so they were cold Pop-Tarts," I admit.

"Breakfast is easy. I'll show you how to scramble an egg and cook bacon perfectly in the oven. You can even use the oven to toast bread or Pop-Tarts, as well," she informs.

"See that's the kind of thing I should know, right?" I ask.

"Should? No, I don't think every woman needs to be a master chef or homemaker. You're a businesswoman. Your work is important and it's hard. I can't operate a computer to save my life. Sophie tried her best to teach me, but it's just not in me. We all have our own talents. You are impressive in your own right. Now, if you want to learn a few kitchen basics, Ria and I would be happy to show you, but don't think you have to."

"I just want to be able to cook a couple of meals."

She smiles.

"Then we'll teach you some of our quick and simple favorites," she offers.

"Thank you, Aunt Doreen."

"Anytime."

We finish cooking and all sit for dinner and I finally understand what Walker has been going on about. Doreen's pot roast melts in your mouth.

Thirty

PAYNE.

"I CAN'T BELIEVE THESE FOUR WEEKS ARE ALMOST OVER," Charlotte says as she snuggles into my side.

"I know. It feels like you just got here," I tell her as I kiss the top of her head.

"Time here always flies by," she muses.

I take a deep breath and decide to lay my heart open. "Why don't you stay?"

She raises her head and looks at me in surprise. "What did you just say?" she asks.

"I said, why don't you stay?"

She lets out an awkward laugh. "That's what I thought you said. You know I have to get back home, silly. Four weeks is a long time to be away from the office. Besides, aren't you getting sick of me right about now?"

I run my fingers through her silky hair. "I don't think I could ever get sick of you."

She sits up and pulls the covers over her. "Payne," she starts, but I don't let her finish.

"I've thought a lot about this, Charlotte. I like having you here, sleeping beside you, waking up with you every morning. I want you in my house. I want to eat dinner with you and watch television with you every night. I want to build forts and plow streets and sled down hills with you … for the rest of my life. I want to build a life and a family with you here."

"Here?"

I sit up and look her in the eyes.

"Yes, in Poplar Falls. Move in with me?" I ask.

"I thought we were just having fun," she mutters.

I feel the sting of the words deep in my chest.

"Just having fun," I repeat.

She nods. "Yeah, I mean, I didn't realize you thought we were heading in a serious direction. I never said I wanted to move to Colorado or that I wanted a family."

"You didn't have to say it. I assumed your feelings were growing, like mine."

She shakes her head. "No. No. That's not what we are about. It's not supposed to be what we're about," she says frantically.

I put my hands on her shoulders. "Calm down. We can talk about this. I know I caught you off guard."

She looks up at me, and I can't read her eyes. It's like she shuttered them, and all the light that usually shines through them is gone. Turned off like a switch.

She shrugs off my touch and stands from the bed. "I should go. I need to … I should go," she says.

"Charlotte, you don't have to leave. Just sit back down and talk to me."

She looks desperately around the floor, not meeting my eyes. "I can't. I can't do this, Payne. I'm sorry." She runs from the room.

What just happened?

I leap from the bed and follow her. She's standing in the entrance of the spare bedroom, where all of her luggage is strewn about. Clothes and shoes hanging half-in and half-out of bags. She's staring at the mess.

"What the hell is going on with you?" I ask, trying not to let anger take hold of me.

I've never been the type to lose my temper easily, but this woman has a way of causing my emotions to boil to the top and run over like no other.

"Me?" she asks incredulously. "You're the one who sprang this on me. We were perfectly fine one minute, and the next, you changed all the rules of the game."

"What game is that?" I ask.

"Us!" she shouts.

"You think I've been playing a game with you this entire time?"

"Haven't you? I mean, we were in this for fun, the good time, the orgasms, right?"

"After all this time, that's how you see our relationship? You think all I want from you is sex?" I ask in disbelief.

"Isn't it? It's not like you've ever inferred that it was anything else. We've never had an actual conversation about being more," she accuses.

"That's unfair, and you know it. I've never treated you like you were just someone I was using to get off. You know me better than that."

"Maybe I don't," she says.

I back away a few steps. Disbelief sinking into my bones.

"Yeah, maybe you don't," I agree.

I stomp down the hall to the mudroom and throw my jeans and boots on. I know I need to walk away before I say something I can't take back. I walk out the back door, slamming it behind me.

I head in the direction of the woods to clear my head.

I reach in my pocket and wrap my hand around the box. I grip it tightly as the baffling conversation with Charlotte rattles around in my mind.

Crazy **HEARTS**

How could I have been so wrong?

I thought we were on the same page. I know what we have started out as a casual fling, just two adults enjoying each other's company from time to time, but somewhere in the past three years, it changed. At least, it did for me. I guess she was still just having a good time.

No. That's not true. I know it, and so does she.

I take the box and open the lid to look at the ring nestled inside. It's huge, over the top, and a bit ostentatious, just like Charlotte. I knew the moment I saw it that it would be perfect for her. I purchased it weeks ago on a whim, knowing we weren't ready for that step just yet, but I was confident that we would be one day.

I close the box, and my chest tightens as I fight back angry tears.

Then, I ball it in my fist, rear back, and fling it as hard as I can into the tree line, watching it sail into the snowy woods.

Then, I turn and walk away.

When I return, she's gone, and so are all of her belongings. There's not a trace left of her, except the lingering scent of her perfume and the bike sitting in the corner of the spare room.

And that damn useless coffee machine. I march to the kitchen island, and I rake my arm across the surface, hurling the contraption across the room and watching it smash into pieces against the wall. The loud crash is a satisfying sound.

I plant both my hands on the cool granite and hang my head.

I'm not a crier—never have been—but as I watch a single drop hit the island, I realize I've just never lost anything worth crying over before.

Thirty-One

CHARLOTTE

"**D**O YOU WANT TO TALK ABOUT IT?" SOPHIE ASKS AS WE drive away from Payne's house.

I called and told her I needed to be picked up as soon as possible. She didn't hesitate. She just assured me she was on her way. No questions asked.

I watch out the window as we pass the apple trees, the barn, the chicken coop, and Marvin and Dottie's charming farmhouse with the white picket fence.

I commit it all to memory, like a photo album of snapshots I file away in my heart.

I'm going to miss this place. I don't think I understood how important it was becoming to me until this instant.

"Charlotte?"

I feel Sophie's hand cover mine, and I let her comfort settle over me.

"Not right now, Sophie," I answer, and she squeezes my hand and drives us back to her house in silence.

Braxton unloads my things when we arrive. I'm still in my pajamas, and he gives me a curious look but doesn't pry.

I follow Sophie inside, and we find Lily Claire in her bassinet in the living room. Their pup, Hawk, is lying guard at the foot of her bed.

I walk over and look down at my sleeping goddaughter, and the crack in my heart erupts and shatters.

Sophie's arm comes around me. We stand and watch her baby girl sleep as silent tears fall.

"I'm going to make us some cocoa," she says.

"That would be nice," I whisper as I swipe at my cheeks.

We spend the day mindlessly watching television while Braxton takes Lily Claire to visit with Jefferson and Madeline. I know he is giving us space to talk but I don't even know what to say. I'm just numb. Sophie doesn't press. She just gives me the silent support I need.

When Braxton returns, he has dinner in tow from Doreen and Ria. Food is the last thing on my mind but Sophie insists I try to eat something, so I take a few bites to appease her. The casserole smells divine but I barely taste it.

I help Sophie clean the kitchen and then she sits up with me for a while longer. I can see that she is losing her battle with exhaustion.

Braxton took the baby and went to bed over an hour ago.

"Go to bed with your husband, Soph," I urge.

"I'm good," she says as she tries to smother a yawn.

"I'm fine. I'm about to turn in myself," I tell her.

She gives in and heads to bed after making sure I have fresh towels and extra pillows in the guest bedroom.

I wash our mugs and turn off the light. As I turn to head down the hallway, I notice the blue file folder sitting on the side table.

I pick it up and carry it to bed with me.

I spend another hour perusing the buyout offer from LG

Unlimited. Then, I fish my laptop out of my bag and hunt down
Robert James's business card.

I awake to the aroma of coffee and the sound of baby giggles.

I sit up and stretch my aching shoulders.

I didn't get much sleep last night. I pushed aside my own battered emotions and dug into the situation with LG Unlimited.

I always do my best work when I'm pissed off or sad. I don't
know why that is, but it's true. You want extra productivity from
me? Make me angry or make me cry. Either one will get the job
done.

I pull on a pair of sweats and a T-shirt, throw my hair in a topknot, and go out in search of coffee.

I find Sophie curled up in a rocking chair, nursing Lily Claire.

"Good morning," I greet as I make my way to the kitchen for a
cup and then join them in the living room.

"Did you sleep okay?" she asks.

"Not really, no," I reply.

"I'm sorry," she offers, not knowing what else to say.

I clear my throat and begin, "I owe you an apology, Soph."

She brings her confused eyes to mine. "What for?"

"For my knee-jerk reaction to the meeting in San Diego and for
making you feel like you had to reject the offer," I say.

She shakes her head in denial, but I stop her.

"It's true. You saw my panicked response, and you made the decision based on my wants and not what was best for you."

I look at the baby and smile. "You're a mom, Sophie. You have
a family to take care of, a ranch to run, and more on your plate than

is necessary. I saw the figure they were offering, and that kind of money would set you up well—set us both up—and it'd free you up to do whatever you wanted whether that was having more children, building a bigger house, or investing back into Rustic Peak."

She doesn't deny it, and I know that I've hit the nail on the head.

"I know you love our little venture as much as I do, and our dream was to build an empire, but that was before you found your home here. Plans can change. They do all the time. I think I was more afraid of losing you than I was of losing the business."

"Why would you lose me?" she asks.

I shrug. "Because you have a new life here that I'm not a part of, and maybe some part of me thought Sophia Doreen Designs was the one thing keeping us linked together."

"That's ridiculous, Charlotte. You're my best friend. The thing keeping us linked is love," she assures me.

"Yeah, I kind of picked up on that last night when I read the file and realized what you were willing to give up for me."

I stand and walk the file over before laying it on the couch beside her. "I did some research of my own, and Robert is right. The value of a company directly correlates the state of the market it's in. Right now, the jewelry industry is strong. The price of precious metals is rising. Our brand name is popular. We should strike while the iron is hot. But something about a buyout still doesn't sit well with me. That's your name. Those are your designs that you hand-sketched. You put thought and heart into every piece we've ever created."

I point to the folder. "I drafted a new proposal. One that sells a majority stake in Sophia Doreen Designs to LG Unlimited, but you'll retain forty-nine percent and continue to keep all creative control. That doesn't mean you have to keep working and designing all the jewelry. It just gives you oversight on who is hired to do the designs and leaves you the ability to keep putting your own pieces out when you feel inspired to. LG will get the other fifty-one percent, and that'll allow them to take over the overall business development of the company. They can expand the brand globally and into new directions, such as exclusive retail sites and other categories, but you will still be the creative lead on product development and marketing because I'm all about you and me becoming the face of the brand. I can't wait to walk down the street and see our faces on a billboard in Times Square."

She lets out a snort of laughter. "Mom would love that," she agrees.

Vivian Marshall would indeed be thrilled to see her daughter, the pride of her life, up in lights. My mother might even brag to her society friends a little.

"We could even feature Mila in an ad campaign," Sophie adds.

Why didn't I think of that? My sister is, after all, a gorgeous, up-and-coming fashion model.

"See, you're already nailing that creative role," I praise.

She sobers. "There's no guarantee that LG will go for this," she says.

"They'd be fools not to. It's an excellent offer. I forwarded a copy for our attorneys in New York to look over as well as one to Stanhope because I know how much you trust and value his opinion. I contacted Robert and gave him the heads-up that we would more than likely be coming in with a counteroffer. Now, I need you to talk to Braxton and for the two of you to take all the facts into consideration—not me or my feelings, but the black-and-white facts—and decide if this is best for you and your family."

She picks up the folder and holds it in the air. "I promise."

We hear the back door open, and Braxton's voice calls out, "You girls ready?"

"Just a minute," Sophie answers. Then, she informs me, "He is taking my truck into Jackie's garage today for service, so he is our ride to the office."

I stand. "I can stay here. It's not like I don't have laundry and packing to take care of."

She shakes her head. "Oh no, you're coming with. You can help me explain some of this to Braxton. Plus, Elle is still out on her honeymoon leave, so I need your help with a few other things and with Lily Claire," she insists.

"I'm all yours."

Thirty-Two

CHARLOTTE

B RAXTON DROPS US OFF, AND WE LEAVE THE BABY WITH Doreen and Ria while we get in a couple of hours of work. Once we get everything caught up for Rustic Peak, we switch gears to Sophia Doreen Designs.

We truly are a great team, effortlessly transitioning from one aspect to the other.

I set up a conference call with Stanhope, a video meeting with our attorney, and send everything we need to the accountant for our meeting when Sophie comes to the city next week, and by lunch, we have conquered our mountain of tasks.

The work helps to keep my mind off matters of the heart, but as soon as I have a moment to myself, I see the look on Payne's face when I told him he was nothing more than a fling, and the ache returns. It's so intense that I find it hard to breathe.

Sophie lets me have my space, but I know that the reprieve is temporary.

Therefore, I'm prepared when she broaches the subject after lunch. We have finished our meal, and she has fed Lily Claire and put her down in Elle's old bedroom for a nap.

Doreen and I are chatting in the living room when Sophie appears in the archway. She's chewing on her bottom lip, which is one of her tells. I brace myself when she takes a deep breath.

"I've given you a day—well, more like a night and half a day, but I've given you time to process whatever you are processing. Now, I need you to talk to me. I've watched you drift off to some painful place and fight tears all morning. You wouldn't let me get away with that shit, and I'm not letting you. So, you might as well spill. What happened at Payne's last night?"

"He asked me to stay," I whisper.

She opens her mouth to start yelling and then stops and closes it, and I can see the wheels turning.

"He asked you to stay? Here, in Poplar Falls?"

I nod.

"That doesn't sound so bad to me. I thought he broke up with you or something, and I was ready to go beat his ass," she states.

"Nope. I'm the one who did the breaking," I mutter my confession.

"Why?" she asks.

"Because I'm not the woman he needs or deserves."

"What are you talking about? You're perfect for him," she exclaims.

I shake my head.

"You love him. I can see it written all over you, Charlotte. It's as plain as the nose on your face. If this is about Sophia Doreen Designs, we'll figure out the logistics. You're not chained to the city. Even if the deal doesn't go through, we have options. We can move the entire operation to Poplar Falls. Hell, if the space in Denver is still available, we can sign a contract right now, or maybe we can consider the full buyout. But don't use our business as an excuse."

"I'm not. I honestly can't move here," I tell her.

"Why not?" Doreen asks.

I turn to her kind and comforting eyes.

"Because ... I can't have children. I can't give Payne the family he wants," I tell them.

"What?"

"I'm infertile. I will never be a mother."

"Oh, Charlotte," Sophie says.

A small cry escapes me.

"What happened?"

"When we were in high school, I started having severe pains in my side and stomach. One night, it was so bad that I was curled in a ball. Mom thought it was my appendix, so she rushed me to the doctor. He ran the tests, and it turned out, it was endometriosis. A severe case, and it had caused scarring that blocked my fallopian tubes. Scarring that couldn't be repaired. They did surgery to help the pain but told me that it would be nearly impossible for me to ever get pregnant," I explain as I wipe tears from my cheeks.

"High school? How did I not know about this?" she asks.

I shrug. "At the time, it wasn't a big deal. I was happy the pain was eased, and babies were the furthest thing from my mind. And I think I was even a little embarrassed. I don't know. I just didn't talk about it. Not with anyone. Even my mother never brought the subject up again. And I accepted it. I would be a mess of a mom anyway, right?"

I look to her for agreement, but all I'm met with is concern.

"In the city, it didn't seem like a big deal. Most of the guys I dated were so self-absorbed that they weren't jonesing to start families. You know how it is there. Everyone is preoccupied with their appearance, social status, and career ambitions to put much focus on other stuff. But it's different here. I'm different here. I see you with Lily Claire and the joy she brings to you and Braxton. I look at Dallas and Myer with Beau and Faith, and I want that too. Payne deserves that, but I can't give it to him, and for the first time, I'm angry. Angry with my body for not being able to do something that it's supposed to be able to do naturally. Angry that God decided that I, at fifteen years old, couldn't be trusted with children of my own. Angry with myself for falling in love with a man I had no business falling in love with, a man who is so obviously meant to be a father, and a man I hurt because I was careless with his heart."

Sophie takes a seat beside me and wraps me in her arms, and I weep into her neck.

"Oh, Char, I'm so sorry."

We hear Lily Claire cry out, and I pull back.

"I'm okay. Go get her. I'm fine."

She squeezes me again and then goes to soothe her daughter.

Doreen is still sitting on the couch, watching me quietly. I forgot she was there.

"Come, Charlotte. Sit with me a minute," she requests as she pats the cushion beside her.

I join her on the couch.

"Did Sophie ever tell you that I had a baby girl?"

"No."

"I did. She died a few hours after her birth. She was born a month after Sophia came along. I was so excited. Vivian was so excited. We were going to raise our girls together. They would be cousins and the best of friends. But my Elise died suddenly. The doctors had no explanation. She just stopped breathing. Oh, there could have been a million things that went wrong. Sudden infant death syndrome covers anything unexplainable when it comes to babies dying.

"I figure God just saw that sweet little one and saw something in her future that was going to be too difficult for her to bear, and he decided to take her before she or I had to suffer it. Whatever the reason, she was gone, and I was broken.

"I never became pregnant again. I don't know why. I think maybe my and my no-good husband's genes didn't mesh. I was angry for a while, angry with myself and angry with God, but as life carried on, he filled my life with babies to love. Lots and lots of them. Sophia first and then came all her friends. Then, Braxton and Elle showed up, brokenhearted and in need of motherly love. Walker too. Dallas came back to Poplar Falls with Beau in tow.

"Now, Braxton and Sophie have made me a great-aunt, and Dallas and Myer have blessed us with another little angel. There are lots of vessels for me to pour that nurturing spirit into. Now, I have a good man who loves me. An enormous family that loves me and who I love with all my heart. My life is full. I could have spent it sitting around, bitter and mad over the one thing I didn't get to have, or I could let that love I had for children overflow into the lives of the ones around me and be thankful for the full life He gave me. The choice was mine. And the option is yours too.

"Don't let this define your life. You have value. You are loved. God will fill that space in your heart if you let Him."

"I know you're trying to help, but I feel like damaged goods, Aunt Doreen. Like I'm not whole, not a real woman."

"Do you see this rug?"

She points down at our feet, and I follow her gaze, confused by the sudden change in topic.

"Yes, ma'am."

"Do you like it?"

I take a closer look. It's a marvelous piece.

"It's lovely."

"It's cowhide. Right here is a flaw in the skin." She draws my attention to a spot near her toe. "Some might think that makes it less than, but you see, the imperfections in the hide are what lets you know it's authentic. Real leather is flawed. Now, I could have purchased an imitation rug, one made of synthetic materials, and it would have been perfect, zero flaws, but it would have been a fake. Anything real has flaws. Anyone real has flaws. People who walk around, acting like they are perfect without scars or trauma, are fake. They are showing you the commercial for their life but not the reality show. You are loved, Charlotte. All of you. Despite your imperfections. They make you … you. And you are a funny, fierce, fascinating young lady."

"Is that enough? Would it be enough for Payne, or would he regret choosing me? He's such a good man. I know that if I told him, he would do what he thought was the right thing. How would I know if he made that choice because he was truly okay with me or because he felt obligated?" I voice my biggest fear. One I've never even admitted to myself.

Humiliation washes over me as I slide from the couch and sink to the floor. I wrap my arms around my knees and rock as the weight of it all crushes me. I've been lying to myself all these years. Trying to convince myself that I never wanted to be a mother anyway. That motherhood was a prison that I wanted no part of when the truth is, I do want it. I want to be pregnant. I want to carry Payne's baby and have it grow inside of me. I want to experience the love that I see when Dallas and Sophie are holding, feeding, and caring for their babies. I ebb and flow between great joy for my friends' happiness and jealousy, and I hate myself for it.

Arms come around me, and I hear Sophie's soft voice as she rocks with me, holding me as tightly as possible.

I'm not sure how long we are there before the sobs start to subside and embarrassment fills me.

"I'm sorry," I whisper. "I know it's silly. How can I mourn over the loss of something I never even had?"

"It's not silly," Sophie assures me. "I wish you had told me sooner. I hate that you've been carrying this alone."

"I think I was afraid that saying it out loud would make it real. Just like admitting that I was falling in love with Payne would make it real. As long as I pretended it was just a fling, somehow, I didn't have to give in to the fear that he wouldn't want me anymore. That he would look at me and see damaged goods."

"That's just crazy talk," Dallas's voice booms from the doorway.

I don't have a clue when she showed up. I bring my panicked eyes to Sophie.

"It's okay. I called her."

"Great," I grumble.

"Don't be mad. I know you're her New York best friend, but you have to remember that I'm her Colorado best friend, and best friends are obligated to tell each other everything," Dallas informs.

I scowl at her.

"It's the rules," she says as she throws her hands in the air, as if it were out of Sophie's control.

"She loves you, and she loves Payne, and the three of us are going to talk through this. You're not alone. You've never been alone," Sophie reassures me.

I bring my eyes to Dallas, and she nods her head in agreement as tears stream down her face.

She walks over and sits down on the floor beside us. "Aunt Doreen filled me in," she says.

"Talk to us," Sophie prompts.

I take a deep breath. "I lost myself in this caricature. Don't get me wrong; I'm a lot, and I know that. I just built on it, you know? If I could convince everyone else that I was more concerned about traveling and work and living this carefree, wild life and that I never wanted a family to tie me down, then maybe I would convince myself one day. And I think I did … for a while. A lie I created in my own mind to make it okay."

"I used to have a friend like you, who claimed to be okay. She hid behind humor and crazy antics, but I could see past her facade.

She walked around angry on the inside. I knew she needed a good scolding, and I knew I could not put up with her attitude any longer. But berating her and yelling at her weren't going to help her, so I put my hands on her face. Told her she was worthy of love, just the way she was. That she was a good human and precious and the apple of God's eye. I told her that I would pray for her to heal. Pray that she remembered that life was beautiful and that she would realize her worth because every day she woke up with breath in her lungs was a new opportunity that was too vauable to waste. Walking around, carrying a burden that made her and the people who loved her miserable. I prayed for her right then and there. Then, I watched as a tear rolled down her face, and she wiped it away. I saw her make the decision to live. Then, I looked her straight in the eyes, in the mirror, and winked," Dallas says.

"In the mirror?"

"Yep."

Dallas clasps my hand and lays her head on my shoulder. "I know you think we can't understand, and we can't fully, but I do know what it's like to mourn the life you imagined. The life you thought you would have. It's an invisible burden. One that's deep inside you that others can't see, but you have to let us in. You have to show it to us, so we can help you carry it. It's the only way you'll heal, Charlotte.

"When my life fell apart, I threw myself into raising Beau. I convinced myself that if I just concentrated on being his mother and nothing else, I wouldn't have to face the disappointment or the fear that I blew it for us both. Then, I realized that I had to let myself off the hook for things that I couldn't control.

"Sometimes, stuff just happens to us. We can either let it destroy any hope we have or we can decide to face it head-on and give ourselves a little grace, knowing that we deserve to be happy—and we can be. It might look a little different from other people's version of happiness, but so what?

"You are uniquely you, Charlotte Claiborne. You can make your own way, and it doesn't have to look like anyone else's."

The three of us sit in silence for what feels like hours. Somehow, their acceptance makes me start to believe that everything will be all right. My two best friends pouring their strength into me.

"You need to tell Payne," Dallas murmurs.

My head pops up, and I bring my alarmed eyes to hers. "No," I say as I shake my head. "I can't. I've hurt him enough. I can't tell him, and neither can you."

"He deserves to know why you ran out on him."

"He'll tell me it's okay. He'll tell me it doesn't matter because he's a good man, but it does matter. I don't want him making a decision out of obligation. I know he wants kids. I asked him, and he told me."

"You should give him more credit than that."

"Please. It's done. Just let it be. Let him heal."

I know that's really unfair of me to ask of her, but I can't tell him. I just can't.

Dallas starts to stand, and I grab her hand.

"Promise me," I plead.

She takes a deep breath. "I promise."

Thirty-Three

PAYNE

I'M SITTING IN THE ROCKER ON MY FRONT PORCH, ENJOYING THE last afternoon sunshine when the caravan arrives. Myer's truck pulls in, followed by Walker and Braxton. They don't say anything as they pile out and stomp up the steps. Walker is carrying a six-pack.

They each take a seat. Myer in the chair beside me, Braxton on the top step. Walker grabs the five-gallon bucket from the sidewalk, throws it upside down, and settles in.

"Fellas," I greet.

"Where've you been?" Walker asks. "I haven't seen you since the wedding."

I slide my eyes to him. "Shouldn't you still be in the throes of marital bliss and too distracted to miss me?" I ask.

"A man has to come up for air at some point, and when he does, he notices if his friends have gone AWOL."

I look to the others. "And you two?"

"Dottie is worried about you. Which means she has Dallas worried," Myer says.

"And Charlotte has been moping around my house and not sharing anything, so that has Sophie worried," Braxton adds.

"Tell me you girls aren't here to gossip?" I ask.

"Nope," Walker says as he tosses me one of the bottles by his foot. "We're just here to have a beer on the porch with our friend."

I catch the bottle, pop it open, and take a long pull.

We sit in uncomfortable silence for about fifteen minutes, and I finally let it out. "I don't know what happened. Charlotte's not a trifling woman. That's one of the things that attracted me to her. She's usually straight up. She was sad it was almost time to go home, and I didn't want her to leave either, so I asked her to stay."

Walker looks confused. "That's it? You asked her to stay, and it pissed her off?"

"Yep."

"That doesn't make any sense. There has to be more to the story," he complains.

I shake my head. "That's everything. I asked her to stay, and she said no. Actually, she freaked the hell out on me. Told me that our relationship was just about sex, packed all her shit, and ran out."

"Everyone knows that's not true," Myer states.

"Apparently it is to her."

"No, it's not. Would she be walking around my house sobbing if that were the case?" Braxton asks.

"How the hell should I know. She wouldn't talk to me and I'm not a mind reader," I tell them.

"Did you tell her you loved her? Women need to hear that. It doesn't matter how much you show them. For some reason, the words are important," Walker tells me.

"I think I did. Maybe not in so many words, but she wouldn't sit down and talk to me and give me a chance to explain."

"Do you love her?" Braxton asks.

"Of course I do. Do you think I'd ask her to move to Poplar Falls if I didn't?"

"No, I don't."

"The question is, do you love her enough?" Myer says.

"What does that mean, enough? What is enough?" I ask, frustrated by the conversation.

"Would you be willing to move to New York for her?" Walker asks.

Me, a New Yorker? I can't even imagine it. I wasn't a fan of the place when I visited there in December.

"And leave my family and farm? The town I love? Give up the business that my father passed down to me?" I ask.

"Yeah, man, for her. If that was the only way to be with her, would you give it all up? Because I would. In a hot minute, if it were Elle, I'd follow that woman anywhere," Walker confesses.

"Isn't it the same thing you're asking of her?" Myer asks.

My chest constricts, as if the air had been sucked right out of my lungs.

Fuck. That's exactly what I did. I asked her to give up everything for me, and I just assumed it would be a simple decision for her.

"I just thought ... I mean, Sophie did it," I try to reason.

"Nah, that was different. Poplar Falls is Sophie's home too. She grew up here. Most of her family is here. It wasn't a question that she'd be the one to move and not me. Rustic Peak is as much hers as it is mine." Braxton shuts me down.

"Shit. I never thought about it that way," I admit.

Braxton stands and clasps my shoulder. "I wouldn't have either, but for Charlotte, leaving New York might be just as foreign a concept as leaving Colorado is to you. She has an entire life there that you don't know that much about. You spent all of two days in the city. She's been there for thirty-four years; of course she's hesitant about uprooting her life. Anyone would be."

"Yeah, sounds to me like you sprung it on her, and then got pissed off when she didn't immediately run into your arms thanking you," Myer adds.

I know they're right.

"It all boils down to if you can live without her, man. Knowing that she's up there, wearing someone else's ring, making love to him every night, waking up with him every morning, making babies with him, and watching them grow. Would you be okay with your girl having all of that with some other douchebag?" Walker lays it out.

No. I don't want that picture in my head.

"You have a lot to think about. We'll get out of your hair, so you can chew on it a bit," Braxton says as he looks at Walker and nods in the direction of his truck.

"Just don't sit here and stew in your own juices like a punk. And answer your damn phone when your friends call you, shithead. What if there was an emergency and Braxton was gored by a bull or something?" Walker throws over his shoulder.

"Shut up, I'd never be gored by a bull," Braxton protests.

"Like I'd be the one? I'm too stealthy," Walker brags.

"No, a bull's just smart enough to know your weak ass poses no threat, so they wouldn't bother," Braxton retorts.

"That hurts, man," Walker says climbing into the truck.

As they drive away, Dallas pulls in beside Myer's truck. He stands, but before he can make his way down the steps, she cuts off the engine and steps out.

"Can you go pick the kids up?" she asks him.

"Sure," he answers.

"Thanks," she says.

He gives her a questioning look, but instead of asking, he just kisses her on the cheek and tells her he'll see her at home.

I stand and walk to the edge of the porch.

"Hey," I say as she approaches.

"Come on, big brother. Pour us a drink. We need to have a talk," she informs me as she marches up the steps and into the house.

Thirty-Four

PAYNE

I LIE IN THE DARK AND WRESTLE WITH MYSELF. AFTER MY conversation with the boys and the bombshell Dallas dropped on me, I know I have some major decisions to make.

I love this farm. I love this land. I take pride in the fact that it was passed down from my great-grandad, to his son, to my dad, and then to me. It means something to me, but it doesn't mean as much as Charlotte does.

I close my eyes and picture what my dreams of the future here look like. The farm, orchard, and cider mill thriving. Visitors from all over the country, coming to spend a few days here with their families, laughing, reconnecting, and enjoying the outdoors and each other. Me and Charlotte, sitting on the rocking chairs on our front porch, watching our own family grow.

The most important part of that dream is her. Without her, the rest doesn't seem to work.

That's the thing about dreams—they can change. You can change.

By the time the sun rises above the white-tipped mountaintops, I know what I have to do.

I get dressed and make a few phone calls, then I set to taking care of the cabin and packing a bag before I head to Dad's.

Both my parents are in the kitchen when I arrive. Mom looks up to greet me and her brow instantly creases in concern.

"Payne, sweetheart, is everything alright?" she asks as she stands to her feet and heads for me.

"How do you do that?" I ask.

"Do what?"

"How do you know when I'm upset before I even say a word?"

"I'm your mother."

It's all the explanation she offers.

I hang my head and take a few deep breaths.

"Marvin, pour us all a cup of coffee," Mom orders, then she takes my hand and leads me to the table.

I sit over coffee and tell my folks that I've decided to move to New York with Charlotte.

Mom's eyes fill with tears and Dad sits silently listening as I give it all to them. I describe what happened when I mentioned Charlotte moving here. I tell them about the conversation Dallas and I had, the one where she filled me in on what Charlotte was going through. I lay it all out on the table.

My chest heavy with the burden of letting my dad down. I'd made him a commitment and I was reneging on it.

"I'm sorry. I never meant for this to happen, but I can't let her go without a fight. If New York is where she wants to be, then that's where I want to be too."

"Honey, we knew Charlotte was the one. We hoped she'd move here with you, but if it has to be the other way around, then so be it," Mom says, trying not to break down.

"Yeah, son, we understand. We'll figure something out. I'm still able-bodied, and I've got a few more good years in me. Between us and Myer and your sister, we'll keep the place running until Beau or Faith are grown, and if they aren't interested, we'll sell it," Dad affirms.

Pain slices through me at the thought of Henderson's Farm and Apple Orchard belonging to anyone but a Henderson.

"It's okay, Payne. You follow your heart, son. God won't lead you in the wrong direction. When He closes one door, He opens another, and we have to be the ones strong enough to walk through it and not turn back," he assures me.

I get choked up as I ask if Dad will take care of closing up and winterizing the cabin.

"I turned the main water valve off, and the pipes just need to be bled. The electricity is turned off. I cleaned out the fridge and cupboards, and I'll get the rest of my things as soon as I'm able."

Mom starts sobbing at that.

I take her in my arms. "It's not like I'm dying, Mom. Just moving. I'll be home for holidays and weddings, and the way that's been going around here as of late, you know you'll see me every other month."

Dad chuckles. "Ain't that the truth?"

"If you learn how to use that cell phone Dallas and I got you for Christmas, you can even video-call me anytime you want to see this handsome face," I tell her.

That makes her smile.

"And just think, you'll be able to come visit and I can show you around New York. I'll even take you to the top of that tower that's in your favorite movie."

"Building," she mutters.

"Huh?"

"It's not a tower. It's the Empire State Building and the movie is, Sleepless in Seattle," she says.

"That's the one," I agree.

She smiles through her tears.

"Handle her with care," she says as she takes my face into her hands, "what she's working through is a hard thing for a woman, and it sounds like she has been avoiding those feelings for a long while."

"I will. If she'll let me," I promise her as I kiss her cheek.

"You'll convince her. Any woman on earth would be blessed to have you, Payne Henderson. My sweet, sweet boy."

She squeezes me one last time and steps away. "You go on now and get your girl," she says, putting on her stern mom face.

Dad walks me out.

"You'll need to send someone for my truck. It'll be parked at the Denver airport. I'll send you the lot number and space. I left my spare key on the island back at the cabin. I also called Dave and told him that you'll be in contact and need him back sooner this year."

Dave is one of our seasonal employees that we furlough in the winter.

"I got it. Call us when you land to let your mother know you made it safely."

I give him one last strong hug.

Then, I climb in and head for Charlotte.

Thirty-Five

PAYNE

I PULL UP THE DRIVE TO BRAXTON'S HOUSE JUST AS THE BACK DOOR opens, and Sophie and Charlotte emerge.

They don't see me as they wrestle with suitcases, and it gives me the opportunity to take her in. She's a beautiful mess, and she looks as bad as I feel. Her hair is pulled back in a short ponytail, her face is makeup-free, and her eyes are bloodshot and puffy.

When she finally manages to get the suitcase over the threshold and out onto the deck, she looks out to the drive and stops dead.

"Whoa," Sophie says, and she plows into her back. "What are you doing—oh."

Braxton walks out behind them with the baby in his arms, and as soon as he catches sight of my truck, he starts grinning. Both women are staring in my direction as he reaches for Sophie's hand. She turns to him, and he somehow silently communicates with her.

She glances back at me and then to her friend with a wary look on her face.

Braxton gives her hand a little tug, and she finally relents.

She says something into Charlotte's ear, and she becomes unfrozen as she turns and nods to her before Sophie lets Braxton guide her back into the house.

That's when I take a deep breath, open the door, and step out of the truck.

She doesn't move as I round the hood and head to the steps that lead up to her.

I stop at the bottom and hold my hand out to her.

"What are you doing here, Payne?" she asks.

Her voice is soft, and it catches me off guard. I'm not used to soft Charlotte. I'm used to crazy, ball-busting, spirited Charlotte.

"I'm coming with you," I say.

She blinks a couple of times and opens her mouth, and then she closes it, trying to process what I said.

"You're what?" she squeaks, and I like that much better than the soft.

There's my girl.

"I said, I'm coming with you. Now, hand me your suitcase. We've got to get all twelve loaded and get on the road. If we hurry, we can still make our flight."

I start up the stairs, and just as I reach her and go to grab the handle of her bag, she shoves it behind her and holds her hand out to halt me.

"What do you mean, our flight?"

I come in closer and look her in the eyes. "I mean that I booked a seat on your flight, and I'm coming with you to New York."

A crease forms between her eyebrows, and she shakes her head. "Why would you do that?" she asks.

"I figure if I'm going to move there, then I need to be on the hunt for a job as soon as possible. Do they have newspapers with classifieds in them, or am I going to have to type up a résumé and use a computer?" I ask.

"Huh?" she asks, still thoroughly confused.

"I'm not great with a computer, but I do know my way around

one. I could take a class or two to brush up on my skills or you can teach me everything you think I need to know."

"Why would you need to find a job in New York? And who in the hell still uses newspaper classifieds? Do you still get a physical newspaper here?"

"Of course we do," I answer.

"Like a delivery boy on a bicycle, delivering the newspaper?" she asks as her eyes go wide.

"We're getting off topic, sweetheart," I say as I try to bring her focus back to the point at hand.

She blinks, as if to clear her mind of the shocking revelation that the *Poplar Falls Gazette* is still in existence.

"You didn't answer me. Why do you need a job in New York?"

"Because I'm not exactly the *kept man* type of guy."

"Stop making jokes and talking in circles and give me a straight answer," she says, and I can see her fire getting hotter by the minute.

"You see, there's this girl who lives there. She's beautiful, funny, sexy, and she has the biggest heart. It's a crazy heart for sure, but I'm head over heels in love with her, and if New York is where she wants to be, well then, I guess I'm moving to New York."

She starts shaking her head. "No, you can't do that."

"I can, and I will," I insist.

"You don't want me," she whispers.

"Says who?"

"I can't give you what you want, Payne. I can't give you a happily ever after with a house full of babies."

"I know," I say.

Tears begin to fall down her cheeks. "You know?"

"Yep, but we'll talk about that later. We have to get on the road."

"I'm not going anywhere with you. You're acting insane. If you know, then what's the point to all of this? You want a family. A big one. Boys to carry on the Henderson name. I can't give you that!"

"Did I ask you to?" I shout.

Her body flinches.

I take a breath and get myself under control. I ask softly, "Did I?"

"No, but ..."

"Just so you know, I'm pretty pissed that you're using my words against me when you are the one who asked questions without giving me all the facts. Had I known everything, my answers would have been different," I continue.

"That's why I didn't tell you," she interrupts. "I wanted the truth. I didn't want you telling me what you thought I wanted to hear," she defends.

"Fuck, Charlotte. The truth? The truth is, I want you. Exactly as you come."

She lets out a small cry.

"Your value isn't in whether or not you can have children. You're valuable because you're you. The rest we can figure out together as we go along."

"How? How do we figure this out? Have your wants changed? Because my body isn't going to. It can't. I'll never be able to give you a Beau or Faith. There are no Lily Claires in my future."

"I don't go around, coveting what isn't mine. That's dangerous. I already have everything I need. That's you. I don't want anyone else's life. I don't want anyone else's home. I don't want anyone else's truck. I don't want anyone else's career. I don't want anyone else's family. I want what's mine. My woman, my home, my farm, and my family. So you can't have babies? Look what you do have. You have friends who love you like you're their blood. I love you. *You*, Charlotte. If you were anybody else but you, I'd have lost interest a long time ago. You're perfect for me, and if God wants us to be parents, we will be. He'll just find a different way. There's adoption, we could find a surrogate, or we could be foster parents. And you know what? If it's not in his plan for us, then we won't. We'll just be a kick-ass aunt and uncle and built-in babysitters for everyone else."

She shakes her head, still fighting me. "It won't be the same. What if you wake up one day and regret not having children of your own? You'll resent me for that. For keeping you from having a real family."

That strikes a nerve. I tamp down my urge to yell again. She's still scared.

"We can have a real family. Look at Myer with Beau. Do you think Myer loves Beau any less because they don't share DNA? Do you think he loves Dallas any less because Beau isn't his biological son? Is that what you think of me? That I can't love a child who's not mine by blood? That I can't love you or that I would think less of you because of something you can't help? Dammit, Charlotte, don't you know me at all?"

She lets go of the handle she's been clutching. Hangs her head into her hands and starts to rock with sobs.

I take the last two steps to reach her. "I love you. All of you. You're crazy as hell, but you're still perfect for me exactly the way you are. I wouldn't change a single thing about you."

"Shut up. Shut up before you ruin it. Take me home, cowboy," she mutters from under her fingers.

I reach up and tug her wrist until I see her eyes. "That's what I've been trying to do, but you're about to make us miss our plane."

"Not *New York* home. *Your house* home," she says, and then she leaps into my arms.

I reach out to grab the railing with one hand and catch her with the other.

She brings her hands to my cheeks and pulls my mouth to hers.

I hold her while she kisses me senseless, and the tension that has had me locked up since yesterday melts off my shoulders.

When she leans back in my arms, I bring my forehead against hers.

"There's a tiny problem. I already had the water cut off at home."

"You did what?"

"I can turn it back on, but it's more complicated than it sounds. I disconnected the well."

Her eyes grow soft. "You were honestly going to move to New York? This wasn't just some big stunt for show?"

I reach into my back pocket and produce my one-way ticket.

She looks it over, and then she shoves me. "Are you insane? You wouldn't last a week in the city. How much was this last-minute ticket?"

"A lot," I admit.

She shakes her head. "Thank goodness you have me to help you run your business. I don't know how you'd make it, spending stupid money like this. I bet your mom wanted to knock you upside the head," she says as she turns and stomps back up the steps.

She opens the door and calls for Sophie.

"Payne and I are going to have to stay here with you guys tonight. You'll never believe what this idiot went and did," she says as she walks in, waving the ticket in the air.

Braxton's head pops out a second later, and he grins. "Get your shit and get in here. We're having tacos for dinner."

I give him a two-finger salute and run down to the truck for my bag as he hauls Charlotte's suitcases back inside.

Wait until she finds out what happened to the fancy coffee machine. The woman is crazy, I think to myself. But she's mine.

Thirty-Six

CHARLOTTE

"ARE YOU NERVOUS?" I ASK PAYNE AS THE CAR DRIVES UP to my parents' front door.

I had Payne's one-way ticket exchanged for a round-trip flight to accompany me to New York to introduce him to my family. It's past time to introduce my cowboy to the Claibornes of Manhattan

"No, should I be?"

I think about that for a minute. My parents are fairly laid-back for New Yorkers. At least my father is. Mom can be a bit high-strung at times.

"I don't think so," I tell him.

"That's comforting," he mumbles as he hands the driver a tip and before helping me out to the sidewalk.

"Here goes nothing," I say as I walk up the stairs to the stoop and ring the bell.

A few seconds later, my father opens the door, and his face lights up when he sees me.

"Charlotte, we weren't expecting you this afternoon," he says as he kisses my cheek.

When his eyes catch sight of Payne standing behind me, he gives me a curious smile before extending his hand.

"Vernon Claiborne," he says as Payne takes his offered greeting, and they shake.

"Payne. Payne Henderson. It's nice to meet you, sir."

Dad's eyes cut back to me, and he steps aside to allow us to pass.

"Come in. Your mother and I were about to sit down for tea."

I lead us into the opulent Upper Eastside home where I grew up and into the sunroom where my parents have afternoon tea every day. Dad and Payne follow as we find my mother setting the breakfast table with scones and finger sandwiches.

"Charlotte, what a pleasant surprise," she squeals. She gives Payne a curious look as she asks, "Who's your friend?"

"Mom, this is Payne Henderson. The guy I told you about from Poplar Falls. Payne, meet my mother, Nova Claiborne."

Payne tips his head to her.

"Ma'am," he says.

Her cheeks turn a slight shade of pink, and she brings her hand to her chest as she speaks.

"Oh, my, call me Nova, please," she says as she leans her hip against the table and accidentally knocks over one of the wineglasses filled with ice water.

"Oh no," she exclaims as she fumbles with one of the cloth napkins to catch the spill.

Dad hurries to her aid.

"It's okay, Mom. Payne has that effect on women. It's the dimples," I say as I turn to him. "Dial it down a few notches, will you, cowboy? She's not used to all that hotness and charm."

Dad barks out a laugh.

"I'll go get two more place settings so you two can join us for tea," Mom says before heading to the kitchen.

"I think that went well," I mumble to myself.

We spend the next hour sipping tea, eating cucumber sandwiches and pate. It's hilarious watching Payne try to covertly sniff each item before he takes a bite, only to grimace a moment later. Mom doesn't seem to notice, though.

I break it to them gently that Sophie and I are selling the majority of our business, and I have decided to move to Colorado with Payne.

Dad seems pleased for me, but I can tell my mother will take her time chewing over the news before I get her honest opinion. That's Nova Claiborne, never one to react until she's had time to process her thoughts.

In the meantime, Dad engages Payne.

"So, you own a farm. I'm not much of an outdoorsy guy myself. I wish I were, but most of my spare time is spent on a golf course."

"That's outdoors, dear," Mom points out.

"Touché," he agrees.

"Say, Payne, do you like to fish?" Dad asks.

"Yes, sir. My buddies and I like to trout fish," Payne answers.

"I bet there is great ice fishing in the Rocky Mountains," Dad surmises.

Payne nods.

"Some friends and I ice fish at Chatfield Reservoir during the season. It's fun, especially at night."

"I'd love to try that someday," Dad muses.

"You're welcome anytime, sir."

"Thank you, son. I'll take you up on that. My buddies and I take an annual trip to Costa Rica. We hire a private boat to take us deep sea fishing. I caught myself a blue marlin that weighed in at over eight hundred pounds. Would you like to see it?"

"I'd love to," Payne agrees.

"Come, he's hanging above the mantle in my study," Dad says as he stands and leads Payne down the hallway.

"Maybe next year you can join us. I've been trying to get Alex down there for years. I bet he'd be on board if you were coming along," I hear Dad offering as he leads Payne to the study.

Mom's eyes follow them.

"Looks as if they have found common ground. I'd say that's good progress," she observes.

We set about clearing the table, and when we make it to the kitchen, I set the dishes in the sink and turn to face her.

"Okay, let me have it," I say.

She places the teapot on the counter and looks up at me.

"Well, I won't pretend I'm shocked. I could see how infatuated you were with Payne when you spoke about him," she starts.

"I can see he is quite smitten with you, as well. And is a handsome devil."

I was nervous, but Payne Henderson swaggered right in and charmed the pants off of my mother. Relief overwhelms me.

"I suppose I'll have to give Vivian a call. Once you're settled, perhaps she will accompany me to Colorado to see where you live and check out this farm."

"It won't be hard to convince her to make a trip to see Lily-Claire. She's locked in a bitter competition with Sophie's Dad's current wife, Madeline, for favorite grandmother," I inform her.

"That sounds like Viv," she muses.

"Yep."

She looks at me thoughtfully.

"Are you positive this is what you want?" she asks.

"I love him. And he loves me. All of me. Even the broken parts," I whisper.

"Oh, Charlotte, you're not broken," she tells me.

"You know what I mean."

"I do, but, darling, you are flawless. An absolute masterpiece."

"Hardly, but I'm going to do my best to be for him," I tell her.

"I have no doubt you'll be great at it. I'm happy for you. If you're happy, but I'm sad for me. All of my babies are flying the nest. I rarely see your brother as it is, and now you're leaving me too," she says.

"At least you still have Mila," I point out.

She sighs.

"Yes, I have my hands full with that one. What will I do without you around to help me with her?"

"I'm working on it. I'm going to offer her my condo so she can get her feet wet living independently, and I've been mentoring her in catching a man."

"Oh God," she says as she throws her head into her hands.

I walk over and pat her on the back.

"Don't worry; you'll like this one," I assure her.

"Who is it?"

"Let's see how it pans out first."

"Fine. I'm probably better off not knowing. How long are you going to be in town? Your father and I would like to take you two out to a nice dinner to celebrate."

"Payne leaves tomorrow. He has to get back to the farm. I'll be here another week or so tying up loose ends, and then Sophie flies in."

"I can't believe you are selling the business," she says.

"I know, but it's the right thing for us. Besides, Payne needs me to help build his empire. I can't wait to start on our plans."

"I guess dinner is out; your father has a late meeting tonight. Is there anything you two need that we can send you?"

I think for a moment.

"Can you teach me how to do laundry?" I ask.

She wrinkles her nose.

"Anything besides that?"

I shake my head. I guess I'll have to rely on Sophie for training. A cowgirl can't have her man's mother washing her dirty undies.

"A new Nespresso machine would be nice."

"That I can do."

Life is full of surprises. As soon as you think you have it all figured out, it throws you a curveball, or ten.

Who would have thought I'd pack up and move to Colorado? Not me, that's for sure.

I only packed the essentials and sent them home with Payne the next day.

Mila is thrilled I agree to let her use my fully furnished condo, and she starts moving her things in before I'm even officially out. I had considered putting it on the market, but I like still having a spot in the city. It will always have a piece of my heart, I'm a New Yorker, but I realized something these last few years; home isn't an address. Home is the place where you feel loved, secure, and at peace. Home is your best friend, your favorite little eight-year-old boy, it's a fiery redhead who will break a promise because she loves you, it's building a better place for the next generation, and loving and being loved by a man who makes you feel like you can do anything. Home is Payne Henderson.

Sophie joined me in the city a week later, and she and I hammered out contracts, met with attorneys and closed up the offices of Sophia Doreen Designs.

It was bittersweet walking out of the meeting where we sold a majority stake in our company, but the timing felt right. Life changes, and we have to learn to be fluid and change with it. Besides, we still own a piece of the pie we baked. The international ad campaign will launch next month with Sophie and me as the face of the brand, and this summer, the very first standalone SDD boutique will open in Tribeca. We will be flying in for the grand opening. It's an exciting new chapter for us, one that frees us up both time-wise and financially so Sophie and Braxton can start working on baby number two, and I can help Payne get the cider mill off the ground. He already has the contractors lined up to begin construction in a few weeks, and he added an office for me to the plans. Lord knows the man needs me. I'll have that place running like a well-oiled machine in no time.

That's enough, for now. Who knows what the future has in store for us? Maybe Payne will get his farm full of kids. Perhaps he and I will grow old and gray and hope Beau and Faith love their uncle and crazy aunt enough to take care of us when we get frail and senile. One thing is certain; I've learned never to say never.

I'll make sure we have enough savings for a kick-ass old folks' home just in case.

Epilogue

PAYNE
Six Months Later

"WHAT DUMBASS THROWS A DIAMOND RING INTO THE woods?" Walker grumbles as he, Myer, Braxton, Brandt, Foster, Truett, Silas, and I march into the mud to try and retrieve the engagement ring I discarded months ago.

"A frustrated dumbass," I admit.

"This is going to be harder than finding a needle in a haystack," he informs me.

"I know, but I have to try. It was the perfect ring, and I can't afford to get another one."

Braxton slaps me on the back. "We'll find it," he assures me.

"Yeah, sure we will. Some animal probably swallowed it already," Walker gripes.

"He helped you build your house before Elle graduated and get the chapel you were married in ready in a month's time," Braxton reminds Walker.

"And I said *thank you*."

"You'll get a *thank you* too—once we find that ring," I tell him.

"Fine. But I'm not digging through bear scat."

"Where are we going?" Charlotte asks as she fingers the silk scarf tied around her eyes.

"Be patient," I whisper into her ear as I guide her down the path.

"Sorry, cowboy, but patience is not one of my virtues."

I chuckle. "Humor me," I demand.

She lets out an exasperated breath as we walk deeper into the trees.

It's a beautiful fall morning. The air is crisp and cool, and the early morning frost is losing its battle with the afternoon sun. The scent of apple blossoms dances around us.

She stumbles, and I catch her before she tumbles.

"Are we there yet?"

"Not quite."

"You aren't taking me into the woods and tying me up to a tree to have your wicked way with me or some kinky shit like that, are you?" she asks.

"No."

"Bummer," she mumbles.

"Maybe later," I whisper into her ear.

"I hate surprises. Have I told you that?" she asks.

"Liar," I murmur into her hair. "You love them."

She melts into me. "I do."

We finally make it to the spot. It's been hard, keeping her from finding out what I've been up to the past few weeks. The woman is exasperatingly curious and doesn't buy any of my bullshit excuses for the late nights and long weekend days spent out here. Sophie and Dallas did their best to help me keep her distracted, but she was onto us all.

"You've been wondering what I've been up to," I start.

"Yeah," she agrees.

"Well, Santa and I have been working together on a very special project."

"Santa? It's September. Are you drunk?" she asks.

"Nope. See, he left the supplies out here and left it to me to do the rest. Me and a few helpers."

Just a few more steps.

"We're here. Are you ready?"

Her body is practically humming with excitement.

"Yes," she shouts.

I reach up and untie the scarf, letting it fall from her eyes.

She opens them and lets out a gasp that echoes through the leaves.

"You didn't," she mutters as she stares at the towering tree house before us.

"Oh, I did," I answer.

She squeals and takes off running to the swinging bridge that leads from the edge of the land and out to the first large branch. From there, she climbs up the winding stairs to the deck of the house, which is nestled in the strong mountain oak that has grown off the side of the mountain and overlooks the river and the back side of the farm.

I follow her up the stairs and find her standing on the deck with her eyes wide and her mouth open in wonder as she slowly turns, taking in the space.

There are Adirondack chairs in front of a propane fire table, looking out to the gorgeous view. A small, wood-paneled two-person hot tub and bamboo yoga mats are off to the left. A wrought iron circle frame holding an impressive supply of freshly chopped wood is to the right.

A wall of floor-to-ceiling sliding glass doors looks into the main floor of the tree house. It has a wood-burning stove with a thick gray shag rug and a wide, low-profile white couch with furry throw pillows. There is a granite island to the side, which has an espresso machine and a small built-in refrigerator and wine cooler that holds twelve bottles. In front of it sits two dark wood stools.

I slide the doors apart, and they open the entire space to the outdoors.

I gesture for her to go in.

Sophie and Dallas helped me decorate the place. There are framed photos of the girls around a bonfire, lamps with woodland shades, floating shelves filled with books, and a small live-edge desk tucked in the corner with connections for her laptop.

Charlotte stands in the middle and looks at every single detail. Then, she walks over to the ladder that leads up to a loft in the turret, which has a king-size mattress with a toadstool table and a reading lamp.

"You built me a castle in the sky," she whispers. Tears fill her eyes as she runs her hand up the side of the ladder.

"I did. Every princess needs one," I tell her. "It even has a lever to bring up the landing at the bridge, so no one can get in unless you want them to."

"A drawbridge. I can't believe you remembered." The tears are streaming down her cheeks now.

"Go ahead, check it out," I say as I nod up toward the loft.

She swipes at her eyes and then climbs the rungs.

I follow behind her, waiting as she crawls up the bed, covered in a plush sage-green down comforter. She falls back on the mattress with her arms opened wide and sighs. Then, she kicks her legs in glee.

"I can't believe I have my own Rapunzel tower!" she yells.

I step up to the end of the bed as she sits up.

"You should see the view from up here," I tell her and gesture to the window above the head of the bed.

She turns and gets up on her knees, and she looks out the window that overlooks the meadow.

"Wow," she whispers, and then I hear her voice catch as she sees it.

The words *marry me* are spelled out in large stones.

"Payne," she says without turning around.

"Yeah, baby?"

"Does that say what I think it says?"

"I don't know. What do you see?"

She turns then to meet my eyes, and I'm on one knee with the open box in my hand.

I raise an eyebrow.

She stares at the ring.

"I guess it does," she whispers through a fresh set of tears.

"Are you going to leave me hanging here?" I ask.

She scoots over to me, still on her knees. She grabs the collar of my shirt and yanks hard.

I fall forward on top of her, and she wraps her legs around me.

"Yes! Yes, yes, yes, yes," she shouts as she peppers my face with kisses.

"Whoa," I say as I lift up and grab the ring that flew out of the box and across the comforter. "We can't lose this thing again," I say.

"Again?"

I pick her hand up and slide it on her finger.

"Never take that thing off. Ever," I tell her.

She doesn't know what I went through to find it. Well, what Walker went through, and the bear.

"Never," she promises, then she fists my shirt and pulls me on top of her.

"Now let's christen this bed, cowboy."

The End

Acknowledgements

What can I say? This book was a labor of love. I had no intention of writing Charlotte's story. I knew from the beginning when she was introduced in Rustic Hearts what her back story would be, and it was not a pretty one, so I kept her on the outskirts, not bringing her fully into the fold. But she wasn't having that, and by the time she arrived in Poplar Falls in Stone Hearts, wearing her ridiculous outfit, I knew she would be a big part of the gang's story. I still fought her and tried to keep her as just the comic relief, but she and I continued to wrestle until she (and the readers) got her way. She wasn't about to go quietly into the night. So, I laid her open for you all, and it was cathartic. I hope I was able to do her struggle justice. Infertility is something that many of us struggle with and acceptance is hard, but it doesn't have to define us. It's not something we need to be ashamed of or to even have to explain. If you are one of those affected by it, you're not alone, and I hope you know how valuable you are. Love comes in many packages and so do families.

Autumn Gantz, as always, thank you for pushing me to write this book and for all your help along the way.

Jovana Shirley, man, this was a rough one. Thank you for helping me get it right and still being my friend at the end. Commas are still the devil.

Judy Zweifel, I appreciate your eagle eyes so much. You catch all the things.

Sommer Stein, it will be hard ever to top this series; I can't wait to see what we do together in the future. Thank you for your creativity.

Michaela Mangum, all I can say is wow. You're an artist.

And as always, last but not least, a big *thank you* to my poor, neglected, amazing, and patient husband, David. I love you infinitely.

Other Books

Cross My Heart Duet

Both of Me

Both of Us

Poplar Falls

Rustic Hearts

Stone Hearts

Wicked Hearts

Fragile Hearts

Merry Hearts

About the Author

Amber Kelly is a romance author that calls North Carolina home. She has been a avid reader from a young age and you could always find her with her nose in a book completely enthralled in an adventure. With the support of her husband and family, in 2018, she decided to finally give a voice to the stories in her head and her debut novel, Both of Me was born. You can connect with Amber on Facebook at facebook.com/AuthorAmberKelly, on IG @authoramberkelly, on twitter @AuthorAmberKel1 or via her website www.authoramberkelly.com.